MATTHEW CROW

Baxter's Requiem

corsair

CORSAIR

First published in Great Britain in 2018 by Corsair
This paperback edition published in 2019

1 3 5 7 9 10 8 6 4 2

A CIP catalogue record for this book
is available from the British Library.

ISBN: 978-1-4721-5331-9

Typeset in Adobe Garamond Pro by M Rules
Printed and bound by CPI Group (UK) Ltd, Croydon, CR0 4YY

Papers used by Corsair are from well-managed forests
and other responsible sources.

Corsair
An imprint of
Little, Brown Book Group
Carmelite House
50 Victoria Embankment
London EC4Y 0DZ

An Hachette UK Company
www.hachette.co.uk

www.littlebrown.co.uk

For Katie, for helping me through
the last steps of the labyrinth.
Consider this one yours.

Mr Baxter was ninety-four years old.

He had three smart suits which he wore exclusively and in rotation, and a first name he would baulk at if used in conversation. He was tall, but stooped the way men of his age do, as if anticipating his imminent return to the earth. He had a thick crop of filthy white hair which he affected into a quiff via pomade and a tortoiseshell comb each morning.

The comb, like Baxter, had survived a world war. And, like Baxter, it had endured a bus crash in Tangier, a socialist march turned looting riot on the streets of Bastille – and a bolt of lightning that decimated his attic bedroom, a particularly resplendent bougainvillea and his neighbour's grey tabby.

The comb was a gift and, unlike Baxter, had enjoyed twenty-nine glorious years with the man who had given it to him.

It was the comb, and its original owner, that Baxter thought of the morning the doctor visited his temporary rooms at Melrose Gardens Retirement Home.

I

'I'm afraid it's not good news, Mr Baxter,' the doctor said, as Baxter sat on the edge of his bed, polishing his glasses.

'Nothing ever is at my age,' Baxter replied with a short laugh.

'What we'd be looking at now is making you comfortable.'

Baxter grunted, replaced his glasses on his head and stared grimly around the room. The walls had been painted a dappled magnolia, and above the bed there hung a crude picture of a country meadow which he found as offensive as the limp meals which were presented to him thrice daily.

'It's like practising being dead and paying for the privilege!' he had announced upon arrival, as his belongings were laid out carefully and to his strict instruction.

He had insisted on bringing with him his record player, a collection of twenty-seven records and a boxful of framed black-and-white photos that he instructed the staff to arrange along the windowsill in a very specific order. It was sentimentality which bound him to his small collections of keepsakes and memories, not necessity. If anything his memory was growing stronger with age. Once hazy recollections had become sharper

3

as he himself began to blur at the edges. All he had to do was close his eyes and off he went.

'Are you OK, Mr Baxter?' asked the doctor, pulling Baxter's attention back to the present.

'Apparently not.'

'No, well, *quite*. It's a lot to digest. Would you like some time? Is there someone we can call for you?'

Baxter shook his head and smiled. 'Do you know,' he said, slowly raising his eyebrows, 'I'm not entirely sure there is.'

Born the only child of a wealthy older couple, Baxter had found youth a bemusing chore and his peers a complete mystery. Then, when orphaned at twenty-one to an arthritic knee, a sensitive accelerator pedal and an inadequately signposted cliff-edge in Dorset, Baxter was thrust into a role he discovered he was made for: that of absolute independence.

Once he'd overcome the gaucheness of youth he developed an easy charm and a willingness for new experiences which endeared him to most people that he met. He made and kept friends both locally and around the world. But the past two decades had seen his social circle diminish incrementally in an inevitable carousel of overpriced wreaths, tuneless hymns and hastily defrosted vol-au-vents. Like some cosmic game of Guess Who? in which he would soon be the only character left.

'Well, there are people we can arrange to come and talk to you.'

Baxter shrugged. 'Nothing to say, really.'

'Like I said,' the doctor went on, 'at this stage there are plenty of things we can do to make you more comfortable.'

'I haven't been comfortable since I slipped a disc in eighty-nine. Why start now?'

'There is medication,' the doctor tried.

At this, Baxter perked up. 'Ooh, yes please!' he said, pointing towards the prescription pad. 'I always was partial to an opioid, none of this holistic nonsense you lot seem to be touting these days.'

The doctor, now very much at Baxter's mercy, began fidgeting with the stethoscope around his neck.

'We often find that the side effects of medication outweigh the symptoms they were prescribed to treat in the first place ...'

Baxter smiled. 'Dear boy. I'm ninety-four years old. And according to your good self I am unlikely to experience the heady rush of ninety-five. What exactly are you worried will happen? *Sweet angel Baxter, gone too soon ...*'

'There's no reason why we can't look at the *possibility* of medication alongside more, ah, *therapeutic* treatments,' tried the doctor, gamely.

Baxter raised his hand the way he used to do in his classroom when the children were getting out of control.

'I apologise for my outburst,' Baxter said. 'It was unfair and disrespectful, and for that I am sorry. But for God's sake, boy, lighten up. Nobody my age sits down in front of a doctor and expects good news. Go off script ... *Relax*,' he said, with a gentle laugh. 'It's only life. You don't always have to take it so seriously. Ask me something normal. Treat me like a human being. There's a roomful of clues and conversational prompts at your disposal.'

'Well, yes,' said the doctor, as uneasy with Baxter's sudden turnaround in mood as he had been with his initial trickiness. There was a long silence.

'Well?' Baxter asked.

The doctor breathed in, scanned the room and widened his eyes apprehensively.

'You going anywhere nice on your holidays this year?' he tried, already shrugging in apology at his effort.

'Bloody hell,' Baxter said, shaking his head. 'Never mind.'

'Is there anything more I can help you with today, Mr Baxter?'

'No. But thank you for your trouble. It has been a particularly gruelling morning. Sixteen across took me three cups of tea and left me with hand cramp from clutching the thesaurus.'

'It's brilliant that you're keeping your mind active,' the doctor said, only to be cut down by a look so sharp it could have shucked an oyster.

'Right then,' said Baxter. 'I shall take a rest. Perhaps lie down with a spot of Mozart.' He stood up and began rifling through his record collection. 'Are you fond of music?'

'I like jazz.'

'So that's a no then,' Baxter said, crestfallen, returning his attention to his vinyl. 'I was always partial to the blues myself. Soul music. And the old masters of course. But jazz ... ' He shuddered. 'Waste of my time and theirs. If you can't carry a tune then learn a fucking trade,' he said with a laugh. 'Don't torture the rest of us with your atonal efforts.'

At this the doctor laughed too, more at the incongruity of such foul language from a respectable old man than anything else.

'Each to his own, eh, Mr Baxter?'

Baxter found the record he was looking for, slid it from its sleeve and placed it on the turntable. The needle hit the groove and a rich melody filled the room like ink in water.

'Thank you for your care and efforts,' said the old man with a nod, as he returned to his perch on the side of the bed.

'You take care of yourself,' the doctor said as he left the room, 'and don't forget to rest.'

'With less than a year left I don't see how I *can* rest,' Baxter said, lying back on the bed, lifting his legs onto a pillow at the end of the mattress. 'There's so much I've yet to do.'

'All in good time, Mr Baxter.' The Doctor said, gently closing the door too and leaving the old man to it.

'It's the most lucrative currency of all, *time*,' said Baxter to nobody in particular, his voice deepening as his body began to sink into his mid-morning nap. 'We must be sure to invest wisely.'

2

Greg Cullock had been working at Melrose Gardens Retirement Home for three days when Baxter arrived.

That morning, like every other, he had woken up in a bed surrounded by remnants of the night before – biscuit wrappers, crisp packets, empty beer cans, well-thumbed novels and an open laptop which buzzed loud and hot against the blankets. Snapping the lid shut, he heaved himself upright and lumbered towards the bathroom.

The house was quiet and still, which meant his father was out at work already. He felt a rare surge of relief. This was pure luxury. He stood in the bathroom in his pants, door open wide. He examined his hair in the mirror and flattened it down with cold water. He squeezed determinedly at a cluster of red mounds that had developed on his chin, wincing and nipping until they popped their entrails across the mirror like pressed garlic. He scrubbed with whatever caustic anti-spot gel had been on offer that month at the local chemist and ran a razor, dry, across his top lip, deleting the tentative moustache which had developed over the past three days.

He'd overslept, and with no time for a shower he filled the basin and spritzed his essentials with a damp flannel and a bar of soap. He stared at his reflection and felt a dull echo of disappointment at the pseudo-stranger staring back at him. He bent down and fully submerged his head in the sink, enjoying the total sensory deprivation.

He pulled up, blinking water from his eyes.

'Fuck,' he said with a start, surprised to see his father's reflection next to his in the mirror.

'Making yourself beautiful?' said his dad.

Greg had known his father for eighteen years and still could not tell the difference between a joke and an insult.

'Just giving the people what they want,' he replied, drying his face as he swigged mouthwash straight from the bottle.

'I nipped back for my spirit level. There's a sandwich on the side for you. Don't be late for work.'

Greg gargled and spat. 'Cheers,' he said, closing his eyes as he wiped his face one last time with the hand towel. When he opened them again his father was gone.

Teddy Cullock was a large man of many trades and few words who had spent the last year complaining about his eldest son to anyone who would listen. Having been self-employed since the age of fifteen, he was known throughout his postcode and upwards of three surrounding environs as a man who could do any job required, so long as you favoured speed over quality. He could build and demolish, wire and lag, paint and sand and tile within reason. Between the hours of eight and six each day Teddy understood himself and his life. His role was clear to him. He could see a problem and a solution, and more often than not had the resources and skill set to connect the two within eight hours, factoring in three tea breaks and forty-five minutes for lunch.

All was not so clear when it came to his children. Initially he had found the role of fatherhood a breeze. Greg and Michael, as babies, had wanted something and he provided it. Yet beyond infancy things had become increasingly unclear. The more vocabulary they accumulated, the less he felt able to communicate. Whatever it was his sons needed from him he did not understand, or more accurately, didn't know how to give. It wasn't that he did not love them, exactly. It was more that he had never been shown *how*. All in all, Teddy felt like an eternal disappointment to his children. They seemed to peel away from him like badly hung wallpaper.

And then Michael died, leaving him and his eldest son more stranded than ever.

Before Michael's death, Teddy had been confused by the very scale of Greg's ambition – his keenness for knowledge, his determination to become whatever it was he was determined to become. The boy was bright. For the past year, however, it was Greg's *lack* of motivation that had mystified him the most. He seemed resigned, if not exactly content, to let the world happen around him.

And so in a desperate effort to stop the rot, he had put in a word with the woman who made him cups of tea when he did odd jobs at the old people's home round the corner, and returned home one evening with an application form and a printed job specification.

'Here you are,' he'd said to Greg. 'Have yourself a shave and set your alarm. You've an interview tomorrow morning.'

*

As the new boy, it had been Greg's job to haul Baxter's belongings from the foyer up to the newcomer's bedroom.

'You should get yourself an MP3 player. Then you wouldn't have this problem,' he'd said, humping the box of vinyl across the thick shag pile.

'And if *you* didn't have an attitude you'd have been done half an hour ago,' Baxter shot back from the wheelchair in which the hospital had insisted on transporting him, despite his protestations.

'As long as you're comfy,' Greg mumbled, as he mounted the record player on the dressing table and dragged a sleeve across his damp forehead. Rugby captain of his school team, swimming champion three years running in the mixed relay, invited to play in goal for the sixth formers whilst he was still in year eleven; yet forty minutes of light labour now left him breathless and dizzy.

'Right then,' said Baxter, wheeling himself around once the task was complete. 'Let's check the damage. I'm sure management can dock your wages accordingly.'

'I feel bloody fine,' Baxter snapped, irritated at the third enquiry as to his wellbeing that morning.

Suzanne ducked behind the great metal urn she had wheeled into the television lounge and released a jet of stewed tea into a cup.

'Well then,' she asked, handing him brew, 'why are you such a miserable old sod?'

She winked. Baxter scowled, though lowered his defences to take two custard creams from the plate his inquisitor had presented.

'Sugar's a poison,' shrieked Elsie from across the room, any notion of appropriate volume dulled by the oversized head-phones clamped to her ears.

'*If bloody only,*' Baxter muttered, taking an elaborate sip of his tea. Suzanne rolled her eyes.

'Not everyone's as lucky as you, you know,' she said to the flinty old boy she'd been lumbered with less than a week prior. 'You've got money – not many can afford to pay cash.'

'Another rapidly depleting resource, let me tell you.'

'Well, old miser, you can't take it with you.'

'Hmph,' Baxter said, taking another sip of his tea and another two biscuits from the plate, 'you haven't seen the coffin I've got planned.'

'Gold-plated, is it?'

'En suite,' said Baxter. 'And anyway, the only reason I'm here is because the alternative was to stay in bloody hospital until the work on my house was finished.'

Suzanne laughed, sighed and flicked the trolley's safety stop-pers with the toe of her shoe. In truth, Baxter was fast becoming one of her favourites within the home. The man was exhausting and infuriating in equal measure, but truculence was a language she understood. Suzanne's forte was giving a shit and the other residents made that hard.

Bobby Braithwaite was a bolter who made a dash for the nearest taxi rank at least twice a week. Violet Melville was a hypochondriac who'd caught the tail end of a *Panorama* on Elder Abuse and would recite the programme word for word on a near daily basis. Peter Oswald was a spitter. Jimmy Golding, seemingly wilfully incontinent. Viv Beasley was a racist and Derek Oswald would stand up and drop his trousers to the floor each day at the chime of the six o'clock news (causing a surge of interest in current affairs amongst the widowed ladies of Melrose Gardens).

Suzanne's breasts had been honked and her bottom pinched. She'd been spat on and sworn at and had her stomach fat nipped by Mary Boyle, who seemed utterly obsessed by 'middle-age spread'.

Baxter, despite his best efforts, was a comparative breeze.

Greg made his way into the TV lounge.

'All right, flower,' said Suzanne. 'You get yourself sorted?'

Greg blushed and ducked his head as all attention turned to him. 'Yeah, thanks. Do you want me to do laundry?'

'You could finish teas off for me if you like, pet. I've got paperwork to be getting on with.'

'Oh, here he is!' Baxter declared. 'The raconteur of Tyne and Wear!'

'*Baxter*,' Suzanne warned him as Greg sloped towards the tea tray.

'Our little ray of sunshine,' Baxter went on. 'Gregory. A good morning to you, my friend.'

Greg bowed his head and shrugged, his cheeks pinking as he took the apron from Suzanne and wrapped it around his work shirt.

'And how are you?' Baxter continued. 'What pleasures has the day brought so far?'

'Cornflakes,' Greg said, kicking the wheels of the trolley into motion. 'You been up the hospital?' he asked, pointing to the blue plaster on Baxter's arm that showed where he'd had further blood tests.

'Heroin,' Baxter corrected him. 'It's an avenue I've been meaning to explore for some time now, and there was a lull during *BBC Breakfast*. I thought to myself, Baxter old boy, it's now or never.'

'Right,' said Greg, continuing on his way. 'Give Suzanne a shout if you think you're going to collapse then. I've not been trained in picking yous up yet.'

'*Trained in picking us up?*' Baxter muttered. 'Lord have mercy.'

Suzanne looked at Baxter and shook her head. 'You be nice,' she said. 'He's a good lad.' Then she yelled across the room, 'I'm just saying. You're a canny lad, our Greg, aren't you, son?'

Greg's shoulders tensed in embarrassment. He shrugged and tried for a smile before getting on with the task at hand.

Baxter waited until Suzanne had gone before he ate his biscuits, one mouthful each, chucked back with the tepid dregs of his tea.

'Greedy guts,' Bert mumbled from the armchair across the room.

'Bugger off,' Baxter mouthed, causing Bert's eyes to widen in alarm and then shut tight, feigning sleep.

'Gregory!' Baxter sang to the other side of the room. 'This could do with livening up,' he said, clanking his teaspoon in the empty cup.

'I'll get round everyone the once before I get to seconds.'

Baxter rolled his eyes. In truth he'd had no desire for the first cup, let alone a second. It was the boy he was interested in.

That Greg was troubled was self-evident. His body and his mind operated on two separate planes – as if he were trying to navigate his own avatar with a faulty joystick. His manner was a salient mix of wilful and reticent; every unspoken retort was writ large on his round, gormless face. That indifference alone did not bother Baxter, but he saw it masked a familiar kind of pain that cools and sets as fury. It was a fury that Greg could not hide, even behind the veneer of indifference cultivated expertly and exclusively by the young. Somewhere along the line life had been unkind to young Gregory. Baxter recognised the wound instantly, like a secret handshake between those left behind. Having little else useful to do with his time at Melrose Gardens, Baxter had made it his mission to find out what had happened to hurt a boy so young – and what he could do to help.

'Good lad,' Baxter said, as Greg refilled his cup. 'And have one yourself, for all your troubles.'

'I'll get done if I have a cuppa before my first break,' Greg said, causing Baxter to sigh at the dearth of youthful revolt. 'You had two biscuits before, didn't you?' Greg asked, checking the tick-chart of names and ailments that lay in a brown puddle atop the trolley.

'Absolutely,' said Baxter. 'Same again, in your own time.'

'You can't have any more. Says Type Two Diabetes here,' Greg said, pointing to the chart.

'Nonsense!' Baxter yelled, causing a small wave of shock around the lounge. 'Doesn't exist.'

'Might want to give science a ring and let them know then,' Greg said.

'Is the attitude free, or will it be added to my final bill?' he asked with an arched eyebrow.

'Sorry,' said Greg, kicking the trolley into action only for Baxter to block his path with his walking stick.

'No, no, don't apologise. If anything it's a relief. I was worried for a while you were completely void of character. I bet you could be quite the little wit if you tried.'

Greg shrugged and smiled to himself. 'I never try.'

This time it was Baxter's turn to smile. 'Hmmm,' he said, checking the coast was clear. 'I can see that.'

'You're very observant, Mr Baxter.'

'You don't know the half of it, sunshine,' said Baxter. 'Suzanne will be at least forty-five minutes by the time she's filled in her paperwork and checked the online sales. Go on, have yourself that cup of tea,' Baxter said, tapping the seat beside him.

Greg checked the door, scanned the room and then poured himself half a cup with two fingers' worth of milk and four sugars. Enjoying his first sip, he looked down at the smart old man with the sharp tongue and the kind eyes before taking a seat as directed.

'So,' he said. 'Now what?'

3

Ramila stood on the pavement outside the retirement home. She swore under her breath as the flame from her lighter caught on her headscarf. She nipped the smouldering fabric with her fingers, drawing hard on the seventh cigarette of her shift that morning.

The heady scent of exhaust fumes wafted from the mechanic's yard to her left, and the thunderous sound of barrels rolling across the pub's gravel two streets back ruined her moment of tranquillity.

'Give a girl a break,' she said to herself, closing her eyes. Two bottles of rosé and a shared bag of crisps for supper last night had not entirely prepared her for the morning shift. Ramila groaned as she felt the relaxation of the nicotine morph into something more pressing towards her bowels.

'Howay in, petal,' Suzanne said, popping her head out of the door. 'I'm about to start teas and I need you on reception.'

Ramila kicked the butt of an earlier cigarette down the drain with the tip of her Nike Air Max as her wristwatch buzzed – she was already halfway towards achieving her daily step target.

'Yes, boss,' she said, giving Suzanne's bum a pinch as she

made her way inside. 'You want a quick tab?' she asked, offering her packet.

Suzanne paused for a moment and shook her head.

'No,' she said with resolve. 'Thank you though, flower.'

'Still quit?' asked Ramila.

'Yeah,' said Suzanne, reaching for the packet. 'I'll just take a couple for later, on the off chance.' She held the door open with her foot and slipped two fags into the top pocket of her uniform. 'Mind, you're glued to that bloody desk until I get back. No breaks. No buggering off. And no radio.'

'Noted,' Ramila yelled, taking out her phone and opening her text messages.

As the eldest daughter of the owner of the Vista Parks Retirement Home Group, Ramila's role at Melrose Gardens was vague not only to her, but also to those she worked for. She had applied for the job on the sly and had broken the news at a dinner for her father's birthday.

Her parents' reactions had been equally impassioned and entirely opposite.

Her mother, Karen Patel, had turned puce with horror. 'I did not,' she said icily, as the waiter cleared small plates from the heaving table, 'bust my balls for thirty-five years so that my daughter could shovel shit in some care home.'

Her father, on the contrary, looked like he'd opened the best present ever. 'I always *dreamed* this day would come,' he said, kissing the top of her head in pure delight.

Ramila smiled and shrugged. 'Family's the most important thing, Daddy,' she said, ignoring her mother. 'If I want to be half as great as you, I have to start learning now.'

Her father beamed at her spiel whilst Karen sat and seethed.

She herself had left school early to begin working as a cleaner, while taking a course in business studies at the local community centre every Wednesday and Friday evening. By twenty-one she'd set up her own cleaning company. By twenty-three she had a staff of over fifty. At twenty-nine she landed one of the biggest contracts in the region – Vista Parks Retirement Homes, over a dozen sheltered facilities stretching from York to Berwick. It was there she met the man with whom she would spend the rest of her life; Vista Parks' owner, Mr Ismael Patel. He gave her a diamond on their first date, a wedding in a castle, a Jacuzzi in the summer house and four beautiful children who thrilled and bemused her in equal measure. Ramila was the eldest and the biggest mystery of all.

Ramila had thought long and hard about how to spin the news, but largely she had taken the job as a means to an end. She enjoyed her life. Pubs on a weeknight and clubs on a weekend; long Sunday lunches with hair-of-the-dog in last night's make-up and fresh pyjamas. But it did not come cheap. Why *not* take a job that required minimum effort and that made her dad happy in the process?

Still, she had definitely chosen to omit certain other key factors that had influenced her decision. The fabricated university acceptance letters, for instance. The hoards of rejections.

The truth was that nowhere else seemed to want her. And in a life of great privilege, this had come as a shock.

Greg arrived at work that morning to find Ramila sitting at reception, wearing headphones and swaying to the beat of whatever she was listening to.

'Morning,' he said, already blushing.

He assumed he'd managed to escape her attentions when, halfway across reception, she'd yelled, 'Stop!' and removed one of her ear buds.

'Talk to meeeeeee,' she said in a low, stern voice.

Greg felt his stomach flutter as he slowed his pace and stood rigidly in place at the front desk.

Ramila had taken him entirely by storm on his first day at Melrose Gardens, by hugging him hello in what had been his first embrace since the lunges of pity at his brother's funeral. She smelled of Minajesty perfume and menthol cigarettes. It was not entirely unpleasant. Still, he had wished the ground would open up and swallow him whole. The problem with people who were comfortable in their own skin, he had come to realise, was that they never seemed to understand just how uncomfortable their cavalier approach could make others feel.

'How's life, Gregory?'

Greg had nothing. He had yet to formulate the basic script for daily interaction. His home life was not a chatty one, and his friendship group had petered to non-existent since he'd been ejected from school. He felt like there was a lifetime of conversation inside of him, somewhere, and hoped that one day he'd find a companion who would encourage it to emerge.

Fortunately, Ramila was a pro at filling in silences. 'Greg,' she said. 'G Unit. The O.G. My diamond. My king. Are you enjoying your time as a valued employee of the Vista Parks Group?'

'Better than stopping in bed all day I suppose,' he said, and Ramila shook her head.

'Incorrect,' she said, taking out a folder from beneath the desk and scanning its contents. 'But I appreciate your attitude.

You know I'm unofficial Morale Manager around here. Is there anything I can do to ease your transition into the life of a part-time care assistant?'

Greg shrugged.

'Come on. There must be something! Company car? Popcorn machine in the coffee room? Stripper Sunday? You name it, I'll look into it.'

Ramila placed her hands beneath her chin and leered forwards, grinning widely.

'What's all this in aid of?' Greg asked, pointing to the scarf. 'Didn't think you wore the hijab.'

Ramila sighed and sat up straight. He was a sweet boy. She liked him and hoped that he knew it.

'Well, Gregory,' she began, 'first let me congratulate you on using the correct terminology.'

Greg checked the clock and saw the minute hand dragging its way towards his start time. He found Ramila's company oddly compelling, if mildly terrifying.

'I'm what they politely refer to as worldly,' he said in his thick Geordie accent.

Ramila smiled and shook her head.

'That's not how they refer to you,' she said with a wink, causing the blood to rise once more in Greg's face. 'Secondly, and I think you'll agree, I have major scarf face. I mean . . . ' she went on, taking her mobile from her pocket, snapping a selfie and showing Greg the evidence. 'Come on!' she said, taking the phone and toying with the settings. 'Have you ever seen such a no-filter-needed face?'

'It's a good face,' Greg said, eyeing the time and feeling his leg twitch as he weighed up whether to make his excuses and potentially offend Ramila – or risk being late for his shift, and incur the wrath of Suzanne.

'But thirdly, and most of all, my grandma is staying.'

'Oh.'

'It's not just for her, though.'

'Good,' he said. 'I like it.'

'Well, don't go liking it too much. I'm not just wearing this for modesty's sake. One glimpse of my beautiful locks and who knows what trouble you'd be in.'

'I'll bear that in mind,' Greg said.

'You just make sure you do,' Ramila muttered, returning her headphones to her ears. '*White devil!*' she yelled down the corridor, as Greg shuffled double-speed towards the staff room.

The residents of Melrose Gardens made their slow migration past Ramila's desk towards the daily morning coffee. Some spoke. Most slouched as quickly as their joints would allow them. Ramila made the majority of the residents nervous. She knew one or two were racist, and she sometimes toyed with them just to make them squirm. Largely, however, they were dull.

She had devised nicknames for them all – partly for her own amusement, and partly because she was useless with names, and faces, and trying. The only name she had fully committed to memory, for some reason, was Baxter's.

'Morning, Mr B,' she said as he made his way towards the lounge. 'You off for high tea?'

'And low company,' he deadpanned, not quite stopping but slowing his already timid pace to make time for the girl.

'You want to stay here and listen to some rap music with me?' she asked, offering an ear bud towards him.

24

'East or West Coast?' he asked and Ramila's eyes widened. Baxter was nothing if not open-minded when it came to the music. Even if he patently disliked the style or sound, he was always interested to know more.

' . . . West,' she tried as Baxter scoffed.

'Then I'm afraid we can't be friends. My loyalties lie elsewhere. Goodbye,' he said, making his way from her desk.

'You always surprise me, Baxter,' she said to his back as he slowly navigated the thick carpet.

'Quite right too,' he said, his voice warm with what she knew to be a reluctant smile. 'I'm an enigma.'

'And a handsome one at that,' Ramila said, watching his shoulders jiggle with laughter as he continued on his way.

4

Suzanne popped her head around the lounge door. Greg was unstacking chairs in the middle of the room. For a moment she remained silent, observing. He was meticulous. The chairs were set in a rough semi-circle with a gap at the front allowing for the day's visitors to take centre stage. Between each seat was left a safe distance for the walking aids and other apparatus upon which the majority of residents depended.

Suzanne liked to see the good in people. In Greg she recognised a sweetness of nature and depth of feeling, combined with a crippling self-consciousness and inability to reach out, that made her feel protective towards him. She loved that he found pleasure in small things – his palpable joy at a midday break, the boyish delight when one of the oldies offered him a toffee. Not one to wear his heart on his sleeve, he nevertheless showed his gratitude in one way or another. The care and attention he paid each menial task was his way of thanking her for taking him on despite zero experience. The unasked-for biscuit he left alongside her morning coffee was a gesture of friendship. The pained smile he gave her each day said,

I'm trying. Maybe one day I'll get there, but for now this is all I can do.

She wasn't sure why she felt so sure of the boy's essential goodness.

Maybe it was his father, who had manoeuvred the boy into working at Melrose Gardens. Teddy Cullock was a brackish fellow whose presence had chilled the room the way her own mother's had done for the first thirty years of her life. Any attempt at humour was met with a cold, metallic clank, like a penny being dropped into a dry well.

More than likely, though, it was what had happened to his younger brother. Dead by his own hand, so the rumours went. The earth still soft above him.

She looked at Greg again. Tears welled in the corners of her eyes. His entire body was tense, primed like a fist as if life had taught him that survival required two skill sets only: attack and defence.

Greg was manoeuvring the final chair into place when a buzzing noise caught his attention from the doorway.

'Shit,' said Greg, dropping the chair.

'Shit,' said Suzanne, blushing as she fumbled with her phone, desperately trying to remember how to transfer a call straight to voicemail.

'Sorry for swearing,' Greg said, picking up the chair and placing it with the others, a little off-kilter. 'I didn't see you come in.'

'No,' said Suzanne, 'well, try to keep a lid on it in front of the oldies. Some of them are only ever four letters away from the ground.'

Greg nodded and stood back, observing his handiwork.

'You've done a smashing job, pet, just the ticket. Have you had a break yet?'

'I'm all right,' he said, hauling the remaining few chairs to the back of the room. 'I only started a bit ago.'

Suzanne shook her head and smiled.

'You'll sharp learn, sunshine,' she said. 'Rule number one round here – never refuse a break or a cuppa when it's offered to you, because they're few and bloody far between, let me tell you.'

Greg nodded at Suzanne but did not smile at her attempt at a joke.

'You settling in all right then?'

Greg nodded.

'And the rest of the staff introduced themselves?'

Again he nodded, by which point Suzanne was out of conversational prompts.

'Well then, why not set up a table with some cups,' she said, snapping the legs of a resting trestle table and angling it firm against a side wall. 'I'll sort out some teas.'

'No bother.'

'Would you like the radio on while you work, Greg?' she asked, tapping the small hi-fi which sat on the bookcase.

'Hadn't thought about it really.'

'A bit of music,' she said, turning the machine on to a barrage of static and hiss. 'What station would you like? Any requests?'

'Whatever you like,' he said, facing the ground as if freshly scolded.

She sighed.

'I won't be here, Greg. What would *you* like?' she asked, raising a finger in anticipation. 'And if you say you haven't thought about it I will ram my boot so far up your backside it'll catch

29

your throat. Have a think of something that would make you happy, and do it. How about that?'

Greg smiled and nodded, walking over to the radio and turning the dial one way then the other, hovering around the ghost of a song until the static abated and a thumping dance track filled the room.

'Used to listen to it on the bus on my way to school,' he said and Suzanne smiled. 'They had a competition every day where if you guessed the song played backwards you could win a hundred quid. I never got it, mind.'

'Never knew the answer?'

'Never entered,' Greg said. 'I still used to be gutted when I didn't win, though,' he said with a shrug.

'There,' she said, 'wasn't that easy? And I got a story out of it too. You're a born conversationalist, my little love,' she said, squeezing his arm. 'Don't be so backwards in coming forwards.'

'Sorry,' he said, reaching out and turning the volume up a notch.

'And don't take the piss, either,' Suzanne said, slapping his hand away from the knob with a friendly wink and a shrug, before returning the volume back to her preferred level.

'Sorry,' he said.

'And stop bloody apologising all the time.'

'Sorry,' Greg said with an almost-laugh as Suzanne shook her head.

'Baby steps, eh? Anyway, you get those cups sorted and then have yourself that break we talked about.' Suzanne made her way out of the room towards her office.

'Thank you,' he said, once she was out of sight.

*

30

Baxter's night had been fitful.

The shy bowel of June Carrow had caused quite the stir at the coffee morning prior. Yet as June's immediate neighbour to the left, Baxter could confirm with certainty that said bowel had not only regained its confidence but found a new lease of life at eleven, quarter to midnight, and ten past two that morning.

Adding to the kerfuffle, Harry Rigby, a loathsome old widower, had twice opened his door during the early hours to holler an expletive down the corridor before returning to his slumber.

Most harrowing of all, and barely half an hour before bird-song, a member of the temp staff had burst into his room armed with a syringe, having misread a name on their chart. Fortunately, this intrusion had not occurred during one of Baxter's intermittent naps, and he was able to ward off his would-be assailant with a few choice words at a volume unbe-fitting the hour.

But Baxter's sleeplessness was deeper rooted. Yesterday's news had not upset him in and of itself – one could not bemoan the prospect of the pall when the years preceding it had been so rich; but it had unsettled him.

For years, Baxter had told himself he had no regrets. Now, all of a sudden, he realised he was wrong. This rare inability to bluff his way through his own feelings was causing a sharp unrest and a sense of great urgency.

The gate to the happiest years of his life had been left cruelly ajar, he saw now, and he needed closure. Nobody reached his age without learning how to say goodbye, but Baxter had been denied the chance to say the one goodbye that really mattered – with the man he had loved above all others.

And he wanted his goodbye. Nothing more and nothing he had not been owed. A real goodbye, so he could rest in peace.

'I feel like I know what I must do,' he told his friend Winnie that morning on the phone, still groggy from his failed attempts at sleep. Winnie had recently been confined to a mobility scooter and he'd caught her on her way to aqua aerobics.

'And what's that, my darling?' she asked, before swearing at a fading car horn.

'Winnie, will you pull over, for God's sake, I can barely hear myself think.'

'I'm running late. This thing is slow. One of the boys in the garage down the road thinks he can wire it to take the speed restriction off. Imagine that!' she hooted.

Baxter sighed and carried on. 'I feel I need go to France.'

'Didn't you get the memo, my love?' Winnie said, pulling in to the sports centre. 'War is over.'

'I'm being serious, Winnifred,' he said and she laughed.

'My darling boy, you must do what you must do. Now, when can I see you? The pub is no fun on my own.'

'Lord knows how long I'll be here, Winnie.'

'Then I shall visit you soon!' she said. 'And we shall talk all about whatever is troubling you then. Must dash – Sheila Clumsky's just whizzed past me and she always gets the good float. Ring me tonight, but not between six and seven because I'm at choir practice.'

Suzanne was welcoming the session musicians at reception just as Baxter made his way downstairs.

'Now then,' she said to the man with a guitar in one hand and

32

some castanets in the other. 'You lot go in the back and make yourselves a cup of tea – we thought we'd start about half past, once we've got a crowd going for you.'

Baxter stopped to let the musicians pass.

'Good morning, sunshine,' Suzanne said. 'How you feeling today?'

'Bloody awful,' Baxter said. 'I tell you what, I'd be healed twice over by now if it wasn't for that mattress. It's like somebody pebble-dashed wet cement.'

A girl Ramila's age, wearing a charity T-shirt and sandals, came in carrying a rain stick.

'They're in the back having a cup of tea, flower,' said Suzanne, pointing the girl in the right direction.

'Who's this?' the girl asked enthusiastically, placing her hand on Baxter's shoulder.

'Oh, this is Mr Baxter. Former music teacher, current bloody nightmare.'

'Insolence,' Baxter muttered.

'Ooooh,' said the girl, 'that's so sweet. Perhaps you'd like to help us out? If you can't manage the triangle you could try the rain stick?' she said, giving Suzanne a knowing wink.

'Bugger off!' Baxter shot back and set off in the direction of the lounge.

'All right, Baxter,' Greg said.

Baxter's face soured at the radio as he made his way to the piano. A quiet beat was pulsing through the room like a headache.

'Do you listen to this intentionally?' he asked and Greg shrugged. 'Music is for enjoyment, certainly. But it's all just so ... predictable.' He sat down at the piano stool. 'Dum ... dum ... de-dum-de-dum-de-dum.'

'They say there's comfort in familiarity, innit.'

'They also say it breeds contempt ... *innit*,' Baxter said, picking out notes on the keyboard before finding a loose version of the song. 'Impressive, eh?' he said, and Greg nodded in agreement.

'We should start a band.'

'Ha!' Baxter yelled, as he continued to tinker away at the keys. 'Between my talent and your charisma we'd be quite the force. Do you know why songs like this are so popular?'

'Because they're fun?'

'That's a matter of opinion.'

'And because you don't have to think about them.'

'Precisely ...' he said quietly, having to concentrate to find the notes which had once poured from him so freely. 'Songs like this work to a formula. See?' he said, maintaining the riff for a beat longer and then improvising his way into another song and another, each with shared DNA. 'Without realising it, from the moment they begin you know exactly where they will end.'

Baxter's fingers finally brought his impromptu jam session back full circle, joining in again with the original tune from the radio.

'Bravo,' said Greg, clapping twice unenthusiastically as Baxter gently bowed.

'Try listening to music that you *do* have to think about once in a while. You might just be surprised.'

'Or I might end up with a headache.'

'Quite the libertine spirit you have,' Baxter said with a roll of his eyes. 'Are you musical, Gregory?'

'Evidently not,' Greg said, nodding towards the radio. 'My brother was,' he said, and then stopped himself.

'Fantastic!' Baxter yelled excitedly, missing Greg's use of the past tense. 'Is he more interesting than you?'

'He certainly was,' Greg said with a shrug, as if trying to dislodge the line of questioning with a slant of his shoulder.

Suddenly Baxter became aware that he had inadvertently waded into dark waters. Greg seemed to curl into himself at the mention of his brother, the past tense still new and sharp on his tongue. Baxter was curious, but had the sensitivity not to press further.

'Well,' Baxter said, 'I should have liked to have met him.'

Greg hung his head.

'Now then, Gregory,' said Baxter. 'I understand tomorrow is your day off?'

'Thank God,' said Greg, relieved to be moving onto safer ground. 'I'm knackered.'

'No doubt,' Baxter conceded. 'Those eight chairs you've redistributed shall take up a gruelling chapter in your memoir, I should imagine.'

'There's more to it than that!' Greg said. 'Believe it or not you're one of the easy ones. I've had to wash the same bedding three times in the last two days. And nobody thanks you for it.'

'No,' Baxter said, 'but they bloody well pay you for it, so stop your moaning. *Anyway*,' he went on, his tone sweeter. 'I take it you've made no plans?' Greg shrugged. 'So how about a mission?'

'Something about that makes me uneasy.'

'Nonsense,' Baxter tutted. 'The thing is, I need to go home.'

'They'll not let you move out until you're better,' said Greg. Baxter shook away his protestations with a flick of his wrist.

'I know *that*. I merely want to pop back to retrieve personal items.'

'More? You brought half your house with you.'

'It's a big house,' Baxter said with a wink. 'I'm an old man and I've a lot of baggage. Come on – you can be my dogsbody. A day at the coast, the smallest of efforts and I'll chuck in a pub lunch if you watch your attitude.'

'How do you know I've no plans?' Greg asked, suddenly embarrassed.

'Call it a hunch. So, is that a yes?'

'No,' he said. 'It's a cautious maybe.'

'Did I mention that Ramila will be driving us?' Baxter said sweetly. 'And I shall be otherwise occupied with sorting through my belongings. How about that?' he said as Greg blushed. 'A bit of sea air, some time alone . . . it's how some of the greatest love stories of our age have started. I should know.'

'Whatever you like.'

'Good,' Baxter said. 'Be here at nine.'

'I'll be here at twelve.'

'Ten,' Baxter demanded.

'Eleven or you can do it yourself,' Greg said, and Baxter was defeated.

'You are bone bloody idle, do you know that?' he said, truly petulant. Baxter was not used to being challenged, let alone falling onto the sharp edge of a compromise.

'So . . .' Greg asked. 'Is that a yes?'

'It's an indignant fine,' Baxter said. 'But I'm not happy about it.'

'You never are.'

'Thin ice, Gregory,' Baxter said and then mellowed. 'Are you finished here?'

36

'Just about.'

'Then I shall take my tea in the conservatory this morning when you have a moment. I should like to observe the scant offerings of the garden whilst the light permits it. Three sugars today. I will need the energy.'

'They say it's a poison,' said Greg, taking his mobile phone from his pocket and checking it on instinct despite months of concrete evidence that no messages would be forthcoming.

'So they say,' said Baxter. 'But do you know what kills more people than poison?' he asked.

'Old age?' Greg replied, somewhere between a joke and a barb.

'*Very good*,' Baxter said. 'But no. Misery. Misery is the most fatal of all ills. I watch you, Greg. Do you know that?'

'I'm a fascinating subject,' he said uneasily, and Baxter nodded.

'I'll say,' he said. 'The world is not out to defeat you, you know. Life is to be enjoyed. Once you lose that thirst it can be impossible to recover. Take pleasure where you can find it, at every opportunity, and life will be either long or happy or both. The rest, my boy, is down to luck.'

Greg nodded. He knew that his misery was conspicuous. He could see it affecting everybody he came into contact with, like trapped odour in a carriage. If only it was as simple as the old man seemed to think. He wished he could claw back his capacity for joy, or happiness, or just plain contentment. If he could tick a box, choose the option, he'd do it in an instant. But unhappiness had come at Greg like a tsunami. He could see no pathway back. His landscape was irreversibly alien now and all he could do was put one foot in front of the other, and hope that one day he'd simply feel *something* again.

Baxter rose shakily from his seat and mounted the walking aid which he'd begun to trouble occasionally since his fall.

'You off, then?' Greg asked.

'Cards,' Baxter said. 'Do you play?'

'Snap, when I was a kid,' Greg tried, and the old man let out a *pffff* sound. 'You'll have to teach me sometime.'

'And I shall,' Baxter said. 'But until then there is a rumour that Harry Rigby is willing to play pontoon for cash.'

Greg smiled. 'Suzanne will have a fit if she finds out you're playing for money.'

'Then she must not find out,' Baxter said. 'Poor woman has enough on her plate, don't you agree?'

'If you say so,' Greg said, returning the chair to its spot in the arrangement. 'Just be careful with your life savings. I don't think Harry's as dumb as he looks.'

'I don't believe in insurance,' said Baxter. 'And with regards to Mr Rigby, well ... nobody on God's green earth could be that bloody thick.' Baxter chuckled to himself as he made his way out of the room. 'But credit to Harry, he gives it a jolly good bash.'

'You going to teach him a trick or two, are you?' Greg asked as Baxter turned once more to face him.

'Actually,' Baxter said slowly, 'I plan on bankrupting him.'

And with that he was gone.

5

Baxter had inherited his parents' estate – three guesthouses along the north-east coast, a small chain of tea rooms, a butchery, a sweet shop and a patch of farmland just outside of Durham – shortly before his university graduation ceremony, where the seats he had diligently reserved for his mum and dad remained empty.

He inherited, too, their modest fortune. A fortune which grew substantially when, before the ink had dried on his credentials, he sold off two guesthouses along the north-east coast, a small chain of tea rooms, a butchery, a sweet shop and a patch of farmland just outside of Durham.

It was not so much that he was keen to demolish all trace of his parents' lives. Rather he was keen to get on with his own. He was older than he had ever been in his life, yet for the first time he could remember Baxter felt young. Fresh out of education, he was ready to work, and keen to begin his vocation as a teacher, hopefully specialising in music. But more than that, he was keen to *live*.

He kept only one property – Lookout's Keep, a deceptively spacious end terrace with a long, thin back garden which opened onto the estuary. The house, Baxter had always thought, would make a fine base for anybody. Lookout's Keep had been the jewel in his father's crown, the guesthouse in which he had been raised amid the comings and goings of travellers and salesmen seeking shelter for the night.

The back bedrooms of the top two floors had almost perfect sea views and the front door opened straight onto the farthest tip of Front Street, a cobbled thoroughfare which seemed eternally decked in bunting, and had almost as many pubs as there were patrons.

The first thing Baxter did as a homeowner was to clear out the majority of his parents' furniture and replace it with exciting new fabrics and laces. The walls were re-papered, and the finest record player known to man took the spot of the grandfather clock in the hallway. The front room was furnished but sparse; just two chairs by the bookstand, with a piano standing tall next to a regimented slew of instruments and songbooks piled high.

Baxter had one true friend. Margaret Milliner, Peggy to her friends, who had known Baxter since birth. By twelve she was the tallest girl in the town and by thirteen had hair so red and a bust so full that she was deemed improper by many, despite her essential goodness. She left school early, working hard for her keep but reading as much as she could in her few spare hours. She watched with glee and envy as Baxter read wider and studied deeper than she'd ever been able to.

Like Baxter she had lost her parents at a young age, though her inheritance was not nearly as grand as his, comprising a two-bedroom terraced house, a grocery store half-stocked, a cash register with two days' takings and guardianship of her young sister, Winnifred, on whom she doted.

As soon as renovations at Lookout's Keep were complete, Baxter had invited Peggy and Winnifred to stay. He and Peggy had sat together in the drawing room and toasted his new life with sherry and records played at full volume while Winnifred snuck from her makeshift bed and listened with glee from behind the upstairs bannister.

'Well, Baxter. You did it,' Peggy said, draining her glass in one, and holding out the empty to her obliging host. 'You're an adult. An actual, functioning adult. Your own house and your new job at the school next term. Welcome to the real world, my dearest,' she said, raising her glass, 'and all that comes with it.'

'To the real world,' he said, raising his glass.

Upstairs Winnifred took hold of Barnaby Bear's soft paw – a gift from Baxter. '*To the real world*,' she mouthed, pretend-clinking a glass with her cuddly new friend.

Downstairs the record changed to a standard which Winnifred had for a long time held as her favourite. She was quick to muffle her excitement, but not before Baxter and Peggy caught a brief yelp of glee.

'What's that sound I hear?' Peggy asked, raising her voice and sharing a smile with Baxter, as upstairs Winnifred's eyes widened.

'Oh, bother,' Baxter said, holding in his own laugh. 'I do hope that's not a *bear* I can hear prowling the landing. I shall fetch the shotgun with haste!'

Winnifred pressed her finger to her lips as a warning to Barnaby.

'Ah,' said Peggy, rolling her head back on the soft velvet of Baxter's new couch, 'it's stopped.'

'Must have just been the wind,' he replied.

'Well, quite,' said Peggy, 'but I must check in five minutes' time, just to be on the safe side.'

Winnifred curled her toes and hugged her knees tight.

'Indeed, but first things first,' said Baxter, raising his glass unsteadily towards his lips.

'This is my last, old boy,' she said, sipping at the drink and swaying woozily to the music.

'But the night has just begun,' he protested as Peggy shook her head.

'For some, maybe.'

'Oh hush. Don't open up tomorrow. I shall pay the difference.'

'There'd be mutiny.'

'Then let them riot,' said Baxter with a wink. 'We shall take shelter by the fire, with cheeses and wines.'

'One day, my love,' she said, 'one day.' And then her face brightened. 'So I take it you'll escort me to the concert hall this Friday,' she asked, standing up and readjusting her hair in the mirror above the fireplace, as she decided once and for all that the lure of sleep was too much to resist.

'What's in it for me?' Baxter asked, though he could think of nothing he'd enjoy more than a night of music and dance with Peggy.

'A chance to be seen on the arm of the finest girl this side of Drury Lane,' she said, rolling her eyes as Baxter remained nonplussed. 'And there's a band playing, five piece. They're from London. Very *exotic*.'

'I'll think about it,' he said, though he knew his answer would be yes. 'Must you retire so early?'

'Some of us,' she said, bending down and kissing the crown of his head, 'have to work.'

'And some of us simply choose to,' said Baxter, topping up his sherry glass.

Peggy made her way towards the staircase. 'Sleep well, Baxter,' she said, as above her Winnifred tiptoed as quickly as she could back to her temporary quarters, throwing herself between the sheets and feigning a deep sleep.

'We should marry,' Baxter said, giddy on the music as he and Peggy spun together in the centre of the dancefloor.

The band had started at a clip and maintained their pace, to the clucking objection of the older revellers. There were five men on stage. Each wore haircuts and tailoring that spoke to edgy, cosmopolitan lifestyles. Their appearance had already caused several ticketholders to retreat uneasily from the hall and Miss Thistle, who owned the bedsit in which they were due to stay the night, to cancel their booking on sight.

The ballroom was heavy with warmth from the bodies and smoke. Low lighting and flickering candles gave the night a dreamlike quality. Seats were rearranged and tables hopped between on the way to the dancefloor, like stepping stones across a stream, as the crowd mingled and made small talk.

Peggy wore an outfit she had reserved for special occasions. Her hair was teased up and secured to her right by a clip in the shape of a rose. Her dress was cut tight at the waist and when she spun it swirled out like coffee stirred with cream. It was the outfit she would wear to a friend's wedding later that year, captured in a photograph that seven decades later would stare out from a gilded frame at an old man in a nursing home.

We should marry. Peggy laughed at his proposition as the band sped faster and faster. She held Baxter's hands and stretched out into the sea of bodies around her, before he pulled her back into his embrace.

'If there's one thing I've learned it's never to trust a man who proposes during a foxtrot,' she said, with a raise of her eyebrow.

'I'm not joking, Peg. You wouldn't have to worry about work. I'd more than take care of you.'

'But I like to work,' said Peggy, as they slowed their rhythm. 'A girl in charge of her own pocket is a girl in charge of her own fate. Besides,' she went on, 'I fear you are suited to a more exciting life than I could ever give you.'

'My dear, you are too modest!' Baxter hollered with mock indignation. 'You've been to Scarborough, have you not?'

They threw back their heads and laughed, still spinning in time to the music.

Later that night in a crowded pub, Baxter and Peggy found a nook and sat down. Peggy placed a cigarette between her lips and looked expectantly at Baxter, who slipped a book of matches from his pocket, lit one and offered the flame.

'Such a well-brought-up young man,' she said, tapping Baxter on the leg as she inhaled and sat back, already feeling defeated by the evening.

In the background someone was mangling the piano with an enthusiasm that outweighed his talent.

'It's the murder of Mozart that tells you it's time to call it a night,' Baxter whispered to Peggy, who nodded in agreement.

'But what a night it was.'

'Our finest yet.'

They were just about to bid their farewells when a man approached their small table with a nod. Peggy recognised him from the band earlier.

'The music man!' she said.

'One of,' he replied. 'I take it you enjoyed the evening.'

'It was perfect,' said Baxter.

'My name's Thomas,' the man said offering his hand. 'Do you happen to be Baxter?'

'Yes.' Baxter nodded. 'Why?'

'I was wondering if I might ask a favour.'

Peggy set about readying her things. 'Baxter can't join your band, I'm afraid,' she said. 'He's swapping the stage for the school room. Isn't that right?'

'I daresay I'm not suited to life on the road,' Baxter conceded, returning his matches to his pocket.

'Well, quite,' said Thomas, reaching out and feeling Baxter's lapel between thumb and forefinger. 'A suit like this must travel only first class.'

'And how about the dress?' asked Peggy as she passed her hands across her fitted form, brave from alcohol and giddy at the handsomeness of the stranger.

'A masterpiece, it goes without saying,' said Thomas, and Peggy did everything in her power not to blush. 'But rest assured I'm not here to ask Baxter to run away with us. Rumour has it you're a man with rooms to let?' he said to Baxter.

'I no longer own the guest houses,' Baxter said. 'Besides, there would be no room for five even if I did.'

Thomas shook his head. 'The others have made arrangements, it's just me left without a place to stay. Would it be a terrible inconvenience to rent a room for the night?' he asked as Baxter and Peggy stood up to leave.

'I'm afraid so,' said Baxter. 'I haven't a bed prepared at mine. We can at least leave you with our seats. If you hang around long enough the landlord may see you and take pity.'

Thomas sat down. 'Well then,' he said, removing his jacket and placing it on the spare seat. 'If you change your mind you know where I'll be.'

Baxter held the door for Peggy. 'Thank you for the music,' he said.

'I'll be here all night,' said Thomas, raising his glass as Baxter nodded and left.

Having seen Peggy safely to her front door, Baxter made his way slowly towards home.

Couples bid him good evening as they passed by. Music from the pubs piped into the night, the noise comforting against the chill of the sea air. With some difficulty Baxter removed the key from his pocket. His feet were sore from dancing and his nerves alive with the music, but his mind kept returning to the music man, sitting alone in the pub, with no place to go.

As it began to rain he sighed to himself, slid the key back into his inner pocket and turned back to the pub, feeling suddenly nervous at his change of heart, but determined that he was doing the right thing.

The room was emptier than when he had left it, the music no more melodic. Baxter scanned the scene for the music man, his eyes lingering sadly on the empty seat where he had left him last.

'Baxter!' cried Molly Gilmore and her fiancé, Benjamin,

with whom Baxter had played chess as a child. 'Join us for last orders,' she said, tapping an empty seat as the landlord rang the bell behind the bar.

'Thank you, no,' Baxter said graciously. 'Thomas, the music man from before,' he asked. 'Have you seen him?'

'Afraid not,' said Benjamin. 'He left not long after you. Why? Has he taken something of yours? Miss Thistle said she felt uneasy in his presence.'

'No, no,' Baxter said. 'I just forgot to tell him something, is all,' he said, bidding the room goodnight as he made his way home in the rain, assuming that to be that.

Baxter woke at the kitchen table to the sound of a knock on the door and the wheeze of a kettle boiling towards dry on the stove top. His body stung from his impromptu nap on a wooden chair as he'd waited for his water to heat. A cup of tea before bed was his go-to for evading the sting of alcohol the morning after. Standing unsteadily, he extinguished the flame and placed the pot onto a cool ring before making his way through the hallway.

'Thomas,' Baxter said on opening the door, blinking and drowsy. 'I came back for you.' He winced as he realised how drunk he sounded.

'So the rumour goes,' said Thomas. 'My circumstances remain unchanged, in case you were wondering.'

'Cruel Fortuna,' Baxter offered.

'She's a dark mistress,' Thomas offered. 'Though I like to think one makes their own luck in this life, to an extent.'

'And to what extent are you hoping your luck runs tonight?' Baxter asked as Thomas shuffled on the spot, spangled with drizzle.

'I thought I'd try, and that . . . perhaps, your short walk home had inspired a change of heart?'

'You're wet,' said Baxter, looking down at the man with the dark eyes and the warm smile.

'Yes,' he said, his smile spreading, his eyes narrowing. 'It's raining.'

Baxter thought for a moment though he knew his reply.

'Then you'd better come in,' he said, standing aside and letting the musician enter.

6

Greg woke early that morning, though his shift did not start until lunchtime.

He smacked his lips in search of moisture, and to extinguish the taste left by the preceding night's supper of chip-shop chips and eight cans of no-brand lager.

He sat up in bed, aware of noise coming from the top landing.

The sound of his father huffing and puffing comforted him only insomuch as he did not need to worry about burglars or ne'er-do-wells. But he felt a cold thump in the base of his stomach when he realised that the activity seemed to be emanating from his brother's bedroom. It was this and only this which raised him from his mattress.

Out in the hallway were several bulging bin bags. The sound of a power drill turned to its lowest setting cut through Greg's mild hangover as he stepped through the obstacle course of memories. He entered the room just as his father was prising a nail from the top corner of a wardrobe.

'What are you doing?' Greg asked. He could tell that his

presence had shocked his father, but Teddy Cullock was keen to hide any trace of alarm. He turned to face his son and nodded a silent good morning, before returning to the task at hand, as one by one the tiny nails dropped to the ground.

Greg rubbed sleep from his eyes and gripped his fists tight, counting to ten on an inhale, and doing the same on an exhale. It was a method he'd learned from his counsellor shortly after his expulsion from school. It was not nearly as effective as the tablets he'd been prescribed, in fact he wasn't quite sure that it worked at all, but it gave him something to concentrate on and allowed him a short respite during which he could order his thoughts.

'Dad,' he tried again.

He approached and put his hand on his father's shoulder.

'*Dad.*'

'This has wanted doing for some time now. No point in putting it off.' Teddy gave the wardrobe a shake to check whether or not his efforts had rendered it flimsy enough to be taken apart with ease.

'But it's Michael's room,' said Greg, scanning the piles of clothes and belongings hurriedly piled on the single bed.

'No ...' his father said, giving the wardrobe a tug, which dislodged the entire left side from the rest of the structure, '... it's not.'

Posters of film stars and bands peeled from the walls where central heating had dried the cheap Blu-Tac, making the faces of his brother's icons stare down at the scene, like angels on a chapel ceiling.

'Why?' Greg asked. 'Why do you need to get rid of his stuff? You never wanted him here when he was alive but you didn't kick him out. Why the hurry to get rid of the evidence now that he's dead?'

He knew the accusations were harsh but deep down, and for the sake of his brother, he wanted his words to hurt.

Teddy remained stoic. His face unchanged, his voice unwavering.

'It's not that . . . I just don't want to have to trip over his shite every time I'm looking for something.'

'What would you be looking for in here? You've not been in since he was in infants.'

'We could use the space,' his father said, turning to carry on with his task as Greg felt the blood rush to his face, barely able to contain the anger welling up inside him.

'What the fuck do you need the space for?' he spat. 'You only ever go to work, go to bed, or pass out in the front room with the lights off getting pissed. We've gone eighteen years without a guest suite. It's not like you've got any friends or family who'd want to spend any fucking time with you.'

'Language,' said his father, meeting his son's eyes coldly.

'Why didn't you ask me? I could have helped you. We could have done it together.'

'Fine words butter no parsnips,' said Teddy. 'Besides – I've not the time to be waiting for you to get your arse in gear.'

Greg sat on his brother's bed and looked around the room. Between the greying underwear and the cracked CD cases he saw Michael's black eyeliner pencil – pilfered by Michael while Greg had distracted the pharmacist with questions about painkillers.

'What do you want that for?' he'd asked his brother on their walk home after a lucrative day's shoplifting.

Greg learned at a young age that he and his brother were in many ways polar opposites, but he loved him no less fiercely for that. Greg approached school like a seasoned professional and sailed through without so much as a thought that it would ever be any different. He was handsome but not jaw-dropping. He was smart but kept his efforts hidden. He was popular but not cocky. He was sporty and well-liked and seldom prone to causing trouble. Greg was what teachers and classmates alike considered A Good Egg. He stood out only insomuch as few children manage to fit in with such ease.

Michael, however, was a one-off. Greg had never known anybody who had come into the world so conclusively themselves, and stayed that way despite the constant attempts of others to convince him to change. He was, as was so often and disdainfully pointed out to him by teachers and relatives, *different*. While the grown-ups around him fretted and wondered what to do, Greg didn't seem remotely bothered.

His character made him a pariah at school and a burden to his family. If anything, at first this only made him stronger. Greg had never known a boy as tough as his brother. Life had rendered him robust in a way most others weren't. Michael had learned the hard way when to fight back and when he was defeated; knowing when to curl up in a ball and ride out the beating was the only way he'd survive the walk home from school. He had a certainty, deep down, that things would get better; that there was a place in the world that was for him, and that this place simply was not childhood.

It was the forensic corrosion of this certainty which had left him a shadow of his former self towards the end.

Though Michael had ultimately taken his own life, Greg held

every person his brother had ever met responsible for his death. Every classmate who'd daubed his locker or tripped him on his way to the hall for assembly. Every family member who'd acknowledge his fresh bruise or ripped uniform with a shrug and a suggestion that perhaps if he started behaving himself he'd have an easier time of it. Every teacher who failed to hide their own amusement when a new nickname was hurled his way during a lesson, or held him partly to blame in the aftermath of a gang beating, for provoking his assailants.

His brother's murder, as he felt it in his heart to have been, was the perfect crime. Michael had been killed slowly and purposefully in a cruel pact by a world bent on extinguishing that which it did not understand. In the weeks following his brother's funeral it was Greg's attempts to avenge this crime which led to his exclusion, ending what everyone assumed would be one of the brightest futures the school had ever seen.

'*A boy needs options*,' Michael had said to his brother with a wink, holding the eyeliner like a precious stone. 'We can't all get by on a short back and sides and a crisp new tracksuit like you. Some of us have to work for our glamour.'

'That shit's not going to help your cause round here much,' said Greg, checking his pockets.

'I don't have a cause *round here*,' Michael said, fishing out a pound coin to pad out his brother's loose change – enough for four cans and ten cigarettes which they would share in a wooded corner of the park. 'I'm just riding out the wave.'

'I wish you'd do it quietly,' Greg said as they reached the off-licence that would serve them beer and cigarettes even with their school uniforms poking out from the neck of their coats.

'So does everyone,' said Michael. 'But they can go fuck themselves. I'm living my life at full volume. I'm getting out of here, bonnie lad,' he said as Greg laughed.

'I know you are.'

'Don't worry, though, young 'un,' said Michael. 'I'll see you right.'

'I know you will.'

'As for the rest of them?' Michael smiled. 'They can eat shit and die.'

'Don't throw his things away,' Greg said as his father continued his careful destruction of Michael's wardrobe.

'Someone may as well have them.'

'*We* may as well have them,' Greg tried. '*Please.*' The desperation in his voice surprised them both.

For as long as he could remember Greg had never asked his father for anything. No help with homework or money for treats. Anything he didn't know he could find in a book or online. Anything he needed he could earn for himself, or acquire via his wits. This gave Greg a sense that he was already his own man; independent and self-reliant and ready to face life head on. As for Teddy, the arrangement suited him fine, anything for a quiet life.

Teddy was reluctant to ever leave a job unfinished but his son's uncharacteristic request struck a chord.

'You bloody well sort it then,' he said moodily, packing away his drill and picking up his toolbox. The wardrobe twitched an inch to the right, before settling at a new, awkward angle. 'I want it done by Monday else I'll take the whole bloody lot to the skip,' he said, making his way downstairs.

Greg sat for a moment, pleased with his achievement but overwhelmed at the task at hand and the responsibility it entailed. In truth he could not face the prospect of throwing out a single item of his brother's. All Greg had left of Michael were memories, a few belongings and one or two photographs. The thought of discarding anything that he had touched brought with it the same chill he had felt that day, when he opened the door to two solemn policemen, inquiring as to his father's whereabouts.

He picked up a book Michael would never finish, still marked at the last page he'd read.

'What you been playing at, bonnie lad?' he whispered tearfully.

Greg felt the room closing in on him. The enormity of the situation, something he was usually skilled at dismissing, seemed to occupy every fibre of his being. The sadness was huge and loud and it would have taken up his whole day, were it not interrupted by a creaking from the wall as the wardrobe wilted, cracked and fell in on itself.

'For fuck's sake,' Greg whispered, and began to laugh, as he stared at the collapsed pile of wood at the far side of the room.

Baxter huffed and tutted as Ramila cleared his cash from the bedspread after slamming down her cards.

'If you'd given me a chance . . .' he objected, as she returned the playing cards to their pack, slipping the crisp notes into the fold of her bra.

'. . . then I'd have beaten you five minutes later,' she said with a smirk, doing a small victory dance with her arms from the comfort of the chair she'd occupied for the last hour.

'Nonsense,' Baxter said, losing the battle to cling on to his own sullenness. 'Anyway, why haven't you brought me any more snacks? I'm perishing here. Virtually a prisoner of war.'

Ramila shrugged and placed the cards into her handbag.

'Perks are for winners,' she said with a laugh.

Baxter knew that for all she was fond of him, he was little more than an excuse for Ramila. 'I'm seeing to Mr Baxter,' she'd protest when Suzanne chased up the progress of fresh towels, or a spillage in the kitchen.

For once he didn't mind.

Baxter's night-time concerns had begun polluting his days and his thoughts, if left undisturbed, pulled him to places he hoped he had long since left behind.

He had learned to work around his grief as best he could. After the war his agony was just another voice in the wail of loss which echoed for years afterwards. But just because the world aches it does not dilute your own sorrows, and the pain Baxter had felt in those empty years, when the world was rebuilt on a flimsy foundation of rubble and gaping holes, had been hard conquered.

Now, so late in the day, his wounds had reopened.

Names he had not mentioned in over sixty years danced on his tongue, daring to be spoken. Names of people that he loved. People that were silenced; their ashes swept clean.

Inside of him were names that deserved to be heard.

Inside of him were names that deserved to be known.

He could not face the prospect of his own demise until he was certain that they would not disappear with him.

Baxter's goodbye would be his final triumph. And he would see to it that he lived long enough to get what was his.

'I shall require your assistance tomorrow, my dear,' Baxter said, as Ramila made her way for the door.

Ramila's heart sank as the old man looked expectantly up at her. Baxter's favours, she had soon discovered, came with a high risk of disciplinary action. Already she had smuggled him in three bottles of red wine, given him the staff Wi-Fi password and risked life and limb standing on his upright chair in six-inch heels and a pencil skirt to remove the battery from the smoke detector in his room. Evidently Baxter would rather risk fiery death than be confronted with the irritating green blip of light every thirty seconds.

Admittedly her position at Melrose Gardens was safe thanks to certain familial perks, but that wouldn't spare her the whip end of Suzanne's wrath if she ever caught her playing fast and loose with the rules and regs. The prospect of that alone was enough to keep Ramila cautious.

'Why don't I like the sound of this?' she asked, and Baxter flapped her concern away.

'Nonsense!' he yelled. 'What more in life could you want than to make an old man happy?'

'That sound you hear is me losing interest,' she said, tapping her foot.

'Very well,' said Baxter, and he smiled. 'That lovely new car of yours . . . it's spacious enough for three, yes?'

7

Greg had not seen the coast in well over a year. The scent of sea air and chip-shop oil reminded him of happy times.

Turning sharply onto Front Street, Ramila lowered the volume on the pounding music. Greg sat up front beside her.

'Will you slow down!' Baxter hollered from the back seat. 'There's no rush.'

Baxter could easily have afforded a taxi home and back and he knew it. He had spent most of his adult life being shuttled from city to coast. The truth was that, in spite of feeling endlessly resentful of his current circumstance, he had come to enjoy the company of Melrose Gardens' youth contingent. Ramila, like all the women he had known, had a relaxed and easy wit that delighted and shocked him in equal measure. He found her presence both familiar and uncertain all at once.

Greg, on the other hand, had whatever came after neurosis. His demeanour was that of an individual attempting to stave off the apocalypse. Yet he couldn't help but like the boy. He was a mystery and a puzzle and, Baxter felt certain, if left uncared for a story that would be over before it had even begun. More to the point, he got the feeling that despite his perpetual rolling eyes and heaving sighs the boy liked him too. Still, Gregory was a defensive soul. Push too hard and he would seal himself off indefinitely. Baxter knew that he had to earn Greg's trust, carefully, cautiously; else he'd be lost to him for ever.

'I said, *slow down*!'

'*Um*,' Ramila said, turning to face Baxter without contemplating the upcoming amber light and sailing through obliviously. 'It's quiz night at the Hussar and I'm getting my eyebrows done at four. We're on a deadline here, sunshine.'

'What exactly are you having done to them?' Baxter enquired. 'They seem fine to me.'

'She's putting a water feature in,' Greg said and Baxter snorted as Ramila slapped his leg.

'That'll do, Sideshow Bob. I preferred you when you were a selective mute,' she said as she ground to a halt behind a slowing van.

Baxter's house looked the way Baxter's house ought to look. This was all Greg could think to himself as they made their way through the wooden doors and into sprawling warren of small rooms. It smelled of old books and stale air, and felt weighted and steadfast. It was, thought Greg as he placed his rucksack onto the ornate floor tiles in the hallway, how Baxter would look if he'd been made of bricks and mortar.

'Hello, old boy,' Baxter said warmly as he made his way down the hall. 'How I've missed you.'

'Ah, it's all right in here, Baxter,' Ramila said, eying the abundance of ornaments and curiosities. 'Were those the stairs you fell down?' she asked, as they made their way past a particularly steep shot of steps leading to the first floor. 'Must have hurt like a bastard, that. I went down on my knees running up with Moira Finkel's insulin and orange juice the other day. Swore the place down, and that was on carpet.'

'Yes,' Baxter muttered, passing his hands across a row of books as he made his way towards the kitchen at the back of the house. 'A glorious memory, my dear. Thank you for the prompt. *Gregory*,' he demanded, 'the kettle on the side there. Fill her up and get it on the stove. I am parched after the terror of my ride here.'

'You'd be more bloody parched if you'd had to get the bus,' snapped Ramila, and Baxter nodded in concession. 'Anyway, you've got some nice stuff,' she said, lifting a blood-red vase to check the print on its base.

'I do all right,' Baxter conceded as he made his way to the kitchen table, where he placed his cane beside a chair, and stared out of the window to the garden and the sea below.

'Who's getting it all when you die?'

'Ramila!' Greg exclaimed, and Baxter chuckled.

'I've got a shortlist of the worthy and the deserving, don't you worry.'

'I should hope so. Just don't forget everything I did for you today, eh? Petrol doesn't come cheap.'

Greg and Ramila had, at Baxter's instruction, buggered off and made themselves useful while he busied himself locating the belongings he'd come for. First off, he'd asked them to open every window that they could locate and let in some fresh air. Next, they were each handed a large glass spray bottle, the labels on which sent Ramila into a flurry of excitement, and instructed to apply two sprays only, no more no less, to each curtain and soft furnishing that they passed.

With a small watering can they made their way through the hallways and into each room, dampening the soil of the pot plants which scattered the house.

'I bet this place is worth a mint,' Ramila said. She eyed each room keenly, as did Greg, though whilst he tried to fill in a character from the evidence he observed, Ramila simply totted up Baxter's net worth. 'There's going to be some flush cat and dog shelter when this old boy dies.'

'I don't think he's an animal lover,' said Greg, turning a small ivory elephant statuette towards the open window.

'I don't think he's a lover full stop,' Ramila added, inspecting a brown leather ottoman shaped like a rhinoceros.

'He's all right really,' Greg said, quietly pleased that the elephant was now able to enjoy the glorious day, and suddenly concerned that the crystal hedgehog it had been watching over was missing out. 'Just different. Hasn't he got any kids?' Greg asked.

Ramila snorted. 'Baxter?' she said, as if privy to a common knowledge which had passed Greg by. 'I think not, somehow. What is it they say ... *a confirmed bachelor.*'

'I suppose,' Greg said, picking two dead leaves from a spider plant and turning it so that the leaves which had been flattened against the wall got their turn in the sun. 'He doesn't really seem like anyone's dad.'

'He's far too cool,' Ramila said.

'Then again, neither does my dad.'

'I know, I've met him,' Ramila offered. 'Fixed the back shower for us. Crispy fellow, isn't he?'

'He's a twat,' Greg said flatly.

'I bet he was a spy,' Ramila said, noticing that Greg's summation of his own father was both weightier and more considered than it ought to have been. 'Our Baxter, I mean. Your dad's just a run of the mill old cowboy, and I'm not talking Stetsons and gay porn parodies,' she said, bringing a muted laugh from Greg.

'He was a music teacher,' Greg said absentmindedly, looking out at waves which glugged at the mouth of the Tyne in the distance. 'Baxter, that is.'

'That's what he wants you to think,' Ramila said. 'He's seen some shit, has Baxter.' She picked up a watch from a bedside table and baulked when she realised that not only was it a Rolex, but a real one at that. 'How many music teachers can afford this lifestyle?' she said, brandishing the watch as Greg scuttled to remove it carefully from her grasp and return it safely to its resting place. 'You could pick any three things from any three rooms in this place and it'd be six months' wages, no doubt.'

'Not six months of mine,' Greg said with alarm. 'How much are you on, anyway? I'm pretty sure what they're paying me is illegal, by the way.'

Ramila shook her head and shrugged.

'I'm very established and competent at my job, Gregory. We all had to start somewhere – you'll reach my lofty heights one day, don't you worry. You've to pay your dues and work your way up, is all.'

'Didn't your dad get you the job?'

'And stop your damn cheek!' Ramila yelled, only half seriously, flicking an elastic band from the writing desk across the room towards Greg.

'Maybe his family were rich,' he said, still uncertain as to whether Ramila's outbursts were as affectionate as he'd like to imagine, and keen to return to a safer, more innocuous disagreement.

'*Or maybe he's a spy,*' she whispered, keen to get the last word. 'I reckon some juicy secrets are going to be buried with our Baxter; maybe you and me can get them out of him.'

Greg moved to the small sash window, unclipped the old-fashioned locks and slid the pane upwards. The wooden frame shot up on its rope winches, releasing a cool breeze that made his skin prickle and his head clear. The garden below was lush and green, with bursts of colour amidst the foliage like bottle-caps in a park field. Beyond, seagulls flocked and caterwauled as they stitched the sky, tracing the emerging tide.

He had spent entire summers on the beach with his brother. With their father at work and money in short supply, they'd get by on wits and charm. If they were careful to avoid the conductor on the metro, having skipped the barriers in town, they could live a good life without spending so much as a penny.

The sea and the sand were free. Drinks would be pilfered from the half-empty glasses left at the pubs along Front Street. Cafés and restaurants would be used when nature called. Food and cigarettes could, more often than not, be cadged from friends they'd make on any given day; folk rendered kinder by warm weather and tepid beer.

As the captain of the swimming team, Greg took his affinity with water for granted. He adored the solitude of the sea. The seeming effortlessness it took to cross great stretches. He liked to swim out as far as he could. He would draw salt water with his powerful arms, flinching as his legs caught on scraps of kelp and unseen creatures beneath the dark surface, until he felt the chill of unknown depth creep up his legs.

Michael was not quite so impassioned by athletics, preferring the pleasure of lazy rays caught wandering along the damp shoreline.

One day they had been walking along the shore together when Michael dropped to the sand and began to roll around.

'Get up,' Greg said, hoofing a small patch of sand across his brother's writhing form with the top of his foot. 'You're covered.'

'Which Madonna am I?' Michael said, oblivious to his brother's unease as the crowd to their left began looking and sniggering. 'Come on.'

'You're a fucking idiot,' Greg said, laughing.

'Wrong!' said Michael, getting to his feet and raising his arms in the air. 'Nil points. "Cherish" is the answer we were looking for.'

Michael shoved his brother playfully, setting Greg off-kilter. Fearing a topple, Greg tried to steady himself. His foot splashed in the shallows as Michael grabbed his elbow to steady him.

'I'm a lifesaver,' he said proudly.

'*You're a dickhead*,' Greg said. Behind them the word *faggot* cast loud and cold from one boy's mouth.

Michael flinched, blinked any trace of concern or unease from his face and quickened his pace to separate himself from the crowd.

'Don't let them get you down,' Michael said to his brother, bumping his weight against his as they reached a safe distance. 'It's not your fault that Dad's poor and your shorts are well gay.'

Greg smirked and shook his head as he tucked his hands into

the garish orange shorts which had ridden so far up his growing thighs that they were little more than glorified underwear.

'You're all man, Gregory. No matter what the haters say. Stand proud!' Michael said, as he upped his pace once more and launched into a set of cartwheels, setting a Catherine wheel of saltwater spraying out around him.

'I hate the beach, me,' Ramila said, standing beside Greg and looking out at the water below. 'You always need a piss the second you get comfy, plus there's always some bell-end with a Frisbee and a bad aim. I can't be doing with it.'

'It's all right,' Greg said quietly, closing his eyes and opening them again, like he was waking from a dream. 'Like anything really. It's what you make of it, I suppose.'

Baxter drained his third cup of tea and refilled the kettle. He felt giddy at his return home. He knew it was temporary, but he chose not to think about that. The moment was his to enjoy.

Most of the belongings he had found within minutes of his arrival. The rest of his spare time had been spent doing what he liked most; pottering about at whim, and unobserved. He had stared out at the garden and watched the first bees of summer zip between plants, overwhelmed by the untouched bounty that lay before them.

In a tidy leather carry-all he had arranged his gatherings. There was a charger for his iPad, as he felt it uncouth to continue relying on Ramila and the many and varied wires which she carried with her always. His passport had been in the kitchen drawer where he kept his stationery and inkwells. He had found, too, his pocket watch, engraved and embossed but stuck on the same moment it had settled upon many years ago. The watch always felt warm in the palm of his hand, even in winter, and its heft pleased him. It had been built to last, and last it had – in form if not in function. What he missed most was its sound; the quiet tick of its heartbeat, which even in its prime you had to press to your ear and hold your breath to catch.

With shaking, heavy hands he unpicked a photograph from its frame and slid it inside the fold of a Moleskine notepad along with a fine-tipped ballpoint pen. Finally, there was the bank card tucked into the small flap within the main body of the holdall.

He sank into one of the cushioned seats of the kitchen table and listened to the patter of feet making their way back downstairs.

'Well, old boy,' he said to the house itself. 'It's been a pleasure as always. Hopefully I'll see you again soon.'

8

Baxter stayed home that summer.

He had intended to travel in the weeks before term started and real life set in. London initially, he thought. After that he was at a loose end – Cornwall, perhaps, or Devon, somewhere near the sea.

His plans all changed the night he opened his door to Thomas.

Thomas, it turned out, was a man without anchor. He lived one chapter to the next, took wide steps with closed eyes and had scant concern for consequence. Life, he told Baxter one night over claret and records, was to be lived; details just got in the way. And having spent his first comfortable night for some months in Baxter's second-best bed, and found inspiration on his morning constitutional to the lighthouse and back along the lapping, hungry tide, Thomas had decided to spend the foreseeable future along the north-east coast.

'The band's taking a break anyway. I could learn some new songs, maybe write some music,' he had informed Baxter at breakfast, mopping the last of his yolk with a crust of bread.

'Perhaps I'll learn how to sail,' he said, and Baxter laughed. 'Maybe I'll paint. The sunrises here are like nothing I've ever seen before.'

Baxter topped up Thomas's tea and allowed the dregs of the pot to stain his own half-cup a darker shade of brown.

'It's often very grey,' he said, offering Thomas the final slice of bread. 'You must have caught us on a good day.'

Thomas thought for a moment and bit into his second helping.

'That must be it. So how lucky it is that I took the chance and came to beg your mercy.'

'Your gall was rewarded,' Baxter said, closing his newspaper. 'I daresay you're not always so lucky.'

'I take it you're not a betting man?' Thomas asked, finishing his breakfast.

Baxter smiled and shook his head.

'I prefer to trace my profits through effort and acumen,' he said, tapping the newspaper.

'That's because nobody's ever taught you the quick route,' Thomas said, *'or the fun one.* I have a deck of cards in my case. I'll show you a game or two later if you like,' he offered.

'Very well,' Baxter said. 'But I only accept payment in cash. You shall not bluff your way to a free night's stay.' He set about clearing the plates.

'Do you know of anybody willing to take on a lodger?' Thomas asked, stacking cups and saucers to minimise Baxter's journeys to and from the sink. 'It won't be for ever.'

'You must stay here,' Baxter said, surprising himself at the offer.

'You certainly make decisions like a gambler,' Thomas said, and Baxter blushed.

'So that's a no then?' he asked, retrieving the last of the crockery as Thomas stood up.

'Not at all. I'd be honoured.'

'Very well,' Baxter said with a smile. 'So long as you're willing to pay your way,' he said.

'I have my showman's fortune to carry me over,' Thomas said and chuckled.

'And after that?' asked Baxter.

Thomas's brown eyes deepened in thought before the answer hit him. 'And after that,' he said, 'is whatever comes next.'

Life on the coast, though simple, never failed to impress Thomas. Few things were as exotic to him as the rhythm and routine of day-to-day domesticity. He would watch with fascination as Baxter readied coals for the fire that evening. He marvelled at the treat of freshly washed and pressed shirts. The way that ingredients became meals – a potato and a slab of butter whizzed into something as luxurious as a bowl of steaming mash – seemed like alchemy.

Evening meals were taken sitting down and dressed properly, often with music, always with wine and lively conversation.

'Delicious,' Thomas would declare, weary from laughter and full of dessert, clinking Baxter's glass in appreciation of his efforts. 'The potatoes, however, made the meal. Expertly peeled.'

'Yes,' Baxter would say, returning his clink. 'Though generally speaking, one is left with more than half the potato when the skin's come off.'

'I only wanted you to have the best part,' Thomas would say and Baxter would laugh. For the first time in his life Baxter felt a pure sort of happiness. Clear and unsullied by his own fundamental reservations.

Wine would lead to cognac and cognac would lead to the record player and then the piano, and before long the pair would find themselves oblivious to the chime of midnight, their shirts unbuttoned, their words slurred, but their timing and rhythm impeccable.

'No, this way,' Thomas would say through a cigarette, leaning over and placing his hands either side of Baxter's on the keyboard, fitting new notes around familiar songs.

Other nights would be more subdued. Weary after a walk from lighthouse to lighthouse and back again, they would sit quietly and read with warm tea. Thomas could not remember a time in his life when he'd had the luxury of doing nothing and he was growing to adore the feeling. He was also falling in love with Baxter's library, and Baxter took delight in guiding Thomas through the collection.

'It's very good,' Thomas said one evening, turning the page of Baxter's latest recommendation. 'Very wordy though.'

Baxter looked up over the rim of his glasses and smiled.

'Yes,' he offered drily. 'It's a book.'

Thomas rolled his eyes as Baxter returned to his text.

And so it was. Baxter was no longer 'I', but 'we'. A landlord with a guest list maxed at one. Peggy would visit as she always had. Though perturbed by Thomas at first, she came to enjoy his company almost as much as Baxter's. Thomas eased Baxter's manner in a way she had not seen before. The pair, individually, were undoubtedly just fine. But together they seemed complete.

*

Peggy took her tea on the patio that morning.

The air was warm, cut through with a clean mist blowing in from the sea. Across the stone slabs which led from the kitchen and through the miniature jungle of his split garden, Winnifred drew hopscotch squares with a hunk of chalk. Baxter was watering the plants, and he chatted away to Peggy as he worked.

It was a long garden but not a large one. His parents had employed a small team of workmen to tend to the space when it had been theirs, but Baxter was different. He felt a rush of pleasure at the gaudy slew of colours he could draw from the dirt, and found comfort in the tilling of earth, the ritual of watering, the bean and the sprout and the leaf and the bloom. It was a pleasure which bemused even Peggy. Her own yard was used only for storing wood and skinning rabbits bought cheaply in alleyways from schoolboys playing truant. But Baxter's garden was his happy place. The house, for a long time, was simply its necessary appendage.

Towards the bottom of the garden, where an old wooden gate led to a path towards the estuary, a noise caught Baxter's attention. It took him a moment to realise that the sound was in fact him being robbed. Someone was taking coal from the shed which stood against the garden's back wall.

Quietly stepping over Winnifred's chalk masterpiece, he made his way back up towards Peggy.

'Whatever is it?' Peggy asked, taking the teapot and warming his cup.

'Jack Bletch is in my coalhouse,' he whispered, as if it were he who was trespassing. 'I think I'm being burgled.'

'It never is?' said Peggy, craning her neck to catch a better look but not interested enough to stand to attention. 'Foul creature.

Take a rake to his face, my darling – the boy needs to learn the hard way.'

It was not the first time Jack had attempted to take what was not his. It wasn't even the first time he'd tried this routine on Baxter himself. He was no longer welcome at Peggy's grocery after an unpleasant to-do over a bar of soap, and the local police could pick him out from a crowd with ease. Jack was more irritant than villain, by and large, yet he was generally accepted to be no good.

'I can see you,' Winnifred said in a sing-song voice, causing a *thunk* as Jack's head hit a beam in alarm. '*Foul creature*,' she added, mimicking her sister.

At this, Peggy made a beeline. Winnifred stood up straight and held her chalk tightly.

'Girls with coarse mouths don't get to grow old,' hissed Peggy, swiping out just as Winnifred skipped lightly forwards out of reach.

'And what of *grown women* with coarse mouths?' she asked, dancing on the spot. Like a housebound dog, Winnifred was always keen for a spat, despite having yet to win such a set-to with her sister and keeper.

Peggy narrowed her eyes. 'Hold your tongue else I'll trade you for stock.'

Winnifred settled back to her drawing as Baxter made his way to the shed door, spade in hand for protection. The Bletches were slow-witted, but famously quick with their fists.

'I beg your pardon,' he said, as Jack emerged from the shed with a heavy burlap sack slung over his shoulder, 'but I do believe you're in the wrong house.'

Jack stopped and his body tensed.

'Are you to chase me from your farm with a pitchfork, Mr Baxter?' he said with a smirk, nodding towards his spade. 'Like a fox?'

'A dog, more like,' said Baxter. 'A flea-ridden hound.'

'We're a community, Mr Baxter. It's the job of the haves to support the have-nots, don't you think?' he said, advancing towards the gate.

'Only the have-nots learn to ask first. Put that back!'

Baxter blocked Jack's path with the spade. Jack paused, but not out of fear. He was quite enjoying the encounter. He turned to Baxter and stepped forwards.

Baxter stepped back on instinct, flushing at the smile spread across Jack's face.

'A dog maybe,' said Jack, stepping further towards Baxter, 'but unlike some, my bite far exceeds my bark.'

Thomas rose late that morning.

Peggy stood up, suddenly more concerned than amused at the dramatic turn the encounter had taken. She was about to collect Winnifred and heed Baxter's request to alert the police, when from behind her the paying guest came marching barefoot into the garden.

'Margaret,' he said with a polite nod. He had been part-way through his morning wash and shave when the noise from the garden caught his attention. His hair was damp and arranged in a loose impression of his customary quiff. 'What is all this?'

'Jack Bletch is stealing from the coalhouse,' she said. 'Baxter is down there reprimanding him. He's asked me to fetch the police.'

'Sit well, Margaret,' said Thomas, and handed her the tortoiseshell comb which he gripped in his right palm. 'And keep this safe until I return.'

'Oh my,' Peggy said, sitting back down as he drove furiously towards the scene of the crime.

'Good morning, Mr Thomas,' Winnifred said, not looking up from her chalk game.

'Good morning, my dear,' Thomas said, his eyes focused on his target. 'A touch of business to attend to and then I shall greet you properly.'

Thomas's vest was wet from his wash, and his shirt was open, held to his body only by the fraying braces which gripped tight at his shoulders. It took half the length of the garden for him to secure the button around his waist so that his trousers did not ruffle down towards his ankles, and all the willpower in the world not to kill the boy who was leering over his friend.

Baxter did not see Thomas so much as gauge his appearance from Jack's change in demeanour. From behind Baxter felt an arm shoot out like a piston. It caught Jack between the chest and the shoulder and sent him sprawling against the garden wall.

'You lousy—' Jack began, only for Baxter to step aside as Thomas leant forwards and hoisted the boy up by the collar.

'Ever so sorry,' Thomas said, flicking his head to rid his eyes of his tumbling hair. 'I believe you've picked up the wrong package. This one is yours,' he said, and popped his fist sharply into the socket of Jack's left eye, causing his body to drop and his voice to rise an octave as he yelped in pain.

Thomas opened the gate as Jack rose to his feet, holding the side of his face in one hand.

'Any other questions?' Thomas asked, picking up the bag of coal from where it lay on the ground.

Jack breathed sharply and looked Thomas in the eye.

'My mistake,' he said eventually, reluctant to be the first to drop his gaze, but smart enough to know when he was beat. '*Gentlemen*,' he said, waving his hand towards the coal as though it were a gift to his hosts, as he made his way from the garden.

That night they played the four hands after a meal of fowl and burgundy.

Side by side on the rickety stool they pounded the keys in harmony, their melody precarious but their intentions clear. A bottle of cognac wobbled on a side table to their right and above them, on the lid, sat two drained glasses and an ashtray in which a smouldering cigarette jiggled to the vibrations of their efforts.

Together they bashed out honky-tonk tunes and standards they both knew by heart. Every so often one would rush ahead so that the other would race to catch up, only for fingers to collide in a tuneless tangle, much to their delight.

Picking at notes as Thomas exhaled his cigarette smoke with an unusual look of contemplation, Baxter found the melody he felt would stretch the night as long as it could last.

'You know it?' Baxter asked, as half a tune rose from his side of the instrument.

Thomas smiled sweetly and set the last half of his cigarette on the lip of the ashtray. His eyes narrowed as he placed his hands and pressed down, meeting Baxter's tune with his until they were as one.

Together they played. The tune was slower than they were used to, and sadder, but beautiful in its own way.

'"Fantasy in F Minor",' Thomas whispered, and Baxter nodded.

'Schubert,' he conceded, slowing his pace to match Thomas's.

The tune meandered on. It had been a favourite of Baxter's for as long as he could remember. Some songs, he felt, moved on tracks. Others, like the one which filled the room that night, could not be contained. It was these songs that he loved the most. Notes, he felt, were winged creatures – the poetry was in their flight.

Thomas, however, did not feel the same.

His tune became slower, more mournful, and before long the notes were spaced out as if spoken by a child just learning to read.

'Is something the matter?' Baxter asked, as Thomas pressed one last note that hung heavy in the air.

Neither looked at the other. Baxter found himself reaching forwards and turning the page of the sheet music simply to provide a distraction from the silence.

It was then that he felt the weight of Thomas's body press towards his side of the piano.

His breath – warm and spiked with liquor and tobacco – rang hot in Baxter's ear, as Thomas kissed him gently and warmly, his lips meeting somewhere between the corner of Baxter's mouth and his cheek.

The room fell silent save the lingering note which Baxter caught with his ring finger as he slid his hands shakily from the piano.

Thomas did not speak.

Neither did Baxter.

For the first time since they'd met they were rigid, as if strangers.

'What made you do that?' Baxter asked eventually, crushing his voice like a ball of paper, so that any emotion was hidden within the folds.

Beside him he felt Thomas shrug and then exhale once, as if to laugh, although he didn't.

'I always was a gambler,' he said.

Baxter nodded. 'Quite the risk to take, don't you think?' he asked, and Thomas nodded in turn.

'I'm sorry,' he said quietly, and again Baxter nodded and sighed.

'So you should be,' he said, closing the sheet music, lifting Thomas's cigarette from the ash tray, taking a drag and handing it over to him. 'I've been waiting weeks for you to do that.'

Thomas took the final drag of the cigarette and stubbed it into the ashtray above their heads.

It was then that Baxter leant gently towards Thomas, and returned his kiss.

'As you were,' he said, pressing his hands into the ivory.

'As you were,' Thomas said, and smiled.

And onwards they played, together.

9

Greg returned from a walk just as the sky was beginning to smudge with orange.

Across the high street, students in groups carried cases of beers and bottles of spirits.

The smell of fat and spice from the takeaways mingled above his head, creating a dull fug which simmered on the warm evening.

He set out aimlessly at first. He had no money in his pocket and no route to speak of, but anything was better than sitting indoors trying to avoid his father.

It was his first Saturday off from work since he had started at Melrose Gardens. It was the best day of the week for most, but to Greg it felt endless and mocking. He knew there would be no buzz of the phone inviting him to a last-minute catch-up; no hobbies to occupy him, or arrangements to keep. There would be no beer gardens or bad jokes or cheap chips devoured with drunken mates in a queue for a shared cab home.

It was true that he had craved solitude since his brother's death. The world had not been kind to his brother, and he had resented the way it kept on turning. Like a child in a room full of adults, he felt neither safe nor comfortable in his new reality and so he did all he could think to do; he quietly and without fuss withdrew.

Recently though, since starting at Melrose, he had felt a change in himself. The forced interaction – unpleasant, largely, but not entirely unwelcome now he was getting used to it – made the loneliness of his days feel as loud as thunder, and something he was keen to avoid.

He walked across the high street and past the houses and well-kept yards on the better side of the road. He kicked a discarded football into an alleyway and waited until it dribbled to a halt before allowing himself to continue. In the park he sauntered past the bandstand and shared a moment with a Rottweiler that had become separated from its owner, before picking his way out past the playing fields and into the trees.

It had not been his intention to end up in the woods. It never was, though recently he found it happening more and more often. Greg stood on a path that if followed properly would lead to a bridge and a walkway across a busy main road. But here, right in the centre, dark and shrouded by thick leaves and heavy branches, the outside world did not exist. Except for the most enthused dog-walker or marathon-trainee, you could almost guarantee solitude.

Greg found the tree easily enough. Around its solid base scraps of police tape lay curled like gift wrap amongst the muddy leaves. Some of the condolence cards left not long after they had cut down Michael's body were soaked through, warped and mushy. Candles in jam jars and the odd soft toy had been stuck into the mud, where three bouquets of flowers lay dead in their wrapping.

He tried to unpick a card from where it lay wrapped around an exposed root. He wanted to know what they had said, what words they had offered long after it was too late. But it was stuck fast and eventually he gave up, balling and flicking the useless strand of paper he'd managed to peel away.

Without realising it, Greg found himself kicking the largest bunch of dead flowers away from the tree into the bushy undergrowth of a sloping bank.

'Oi!' yelled a voice from behind him. Greg turned round sharply. A man stood glaring at him, a muzzled greyhound by his side. 'You should respect the dead,' he said, his voice less harsh this time.

Very well, Greg found himself thinking in Baxter's voice, *but what of the living?*

'You don't know shit,' he said quietly.

The man walked off and Greg watched him go.

He felt the sadness well up inside of him on his walk home. The only thing lonelier than solitude is the cold silence of another. His father, he knew, would either be mute or asleep, surrounded by a depleting pile of cigarettes and beer cans.

He wanted to stand there and cry. Not just cry but wail. He wanted to throw a tantrum right there on the high street. To lie down in the road and spread like a starfish. He did not wish for death. For all Greg found no pleasure in life, the uncertainty of the alternative scared him enough to keep him right where he was. Rather, he wanted to cause an obstruction – to inhibit and unsettle the thrust of the world around him. He wanted to rip out his insides and show passers-by; to hand them out piece by ugly piece, to share his burden for once.

A text message interrupted his thoughts.

New Message

All right bonnie lad. How's tricks? Just so you know I've
been cracked onto twice already and I'm barely onto
my second bottle of wine, therefore my eyebrows are
perfect. Lots of love, your friend with hugely on-point
facial hair, Ramila Xx

He went to reply but his phone buzzed again in his hands.

New Message

Ps. Suzanne is kicking right off because Baxter
reckons he's off to France. She said over my dead
body and he said if needs be. Should have seen her
face. I was like GET IN SON and now she reckons
she's gonna put me on a disciplinary for encouraging
insubordination or some shit YOLO xx

He smiled and hit reply only for his phone to buzz once more.

New Message

PPS. Someone's been pissing in the plant pot by the
first-floor lift LOLOLOLOLOLOLOLOLOLOLOLOLOLOLOL x

Greg placed his phone in the pocket of his hoodie. Again
he found himself wanting to cry, but this time with happiness, the way he thought happened only in films. He tried to
think back but could not remember the last time his phone
had alerted him to a message sent through care or concern,
rather than to inform him of an unpaid bill, or the latest
lunchtime offer at the takeaway companies to whom he owed

his current physique. He smiled at the gesture and he smiled at the words. She was joking, of course, but she had said it and she had meant it.

Your friend.

His reply must make her laugh effortlessly. He must strike the right tone, perhaps try to stretch the initial theme, or develop an in-joke he could always fall back on if ever he felt conversation becoming strained between the pair. The thought would carry him well into the night.

Your friend . . .

He thought to himself, playing the words over and over in his head, as the red man turned green, and Greg crossed the road; heavy, still, but a little bit lighter.

His good mood was to be short-lived. Rounding the corner onto his street he was greeted by the sight of a row of black bin bags placed along the front wall of their house. Greg picked up his pace, opened one of the bags, sat on his haunches and dug through the contents. Michael's belongings. Not everything he'd owned, Greg was pleased to discover, but it was everything he had ever worn.

Greg left the front door hanging open as he ran upstairs to check on his brother's room. Broken hangers and scraps of flint scattered the carpet. The bed was once more recognisable as a bed, now that the piles of clothes had been removed. Fortunately everything else remained in situ. His father's efforts had clearly been cut short by the lure of the bottle and for once Greg felt grateful.

'Why did you do that?' he asked, squinting to see through the cigarette smoke in the sealed front room.

His father was slumped on the sofa. The lights were off and

the curtains closed, the only light emanating was from the TV, which played on mute.

His father, though never a young-looking man, seemed older than ever. He looked tough and wizened, like a piece of meat being cured at double speed.

'Had to happen sometime,' he said without looking at Greg, 'and you're always off gallivanting. Who else would do it?'

'Give me a break. I've been out twice. Twice in the last two days. Twice in the last eighteen months.'

'You can make your way through the rest this week.'

'I wanted to make my way through it all. Why have you just chucked it out? It's no tidier out there than it was before. Who do you think is going to collect it?'

'Not my problem any more.'

'Yes,' Greg said, 'it is. Why did you do that? Was it just to get at me?'

'Well, don't we think a lot of ourselves this evening?'

'You've literally achieved nothing by doing it. You've shifted shite from one spot to another. It can't even go to charity now it's so fucked.'

There was a long pause as Teddy cleared his throat. 'What do you want from me?' he asked in a voice thick with alcohol.

Greg wiped a single tear from his eye and forced his emotion deep down inside of himself.

'I just,' he tried, 'I just want you to be there for me,' he said limply, and his father snorted.

'I'm always bloody here. Fat chance I've got of having a night out for myself.'

'I don't mean on the sofa, you stupid fuck,' Greg said, and his father made the sound of an engine revving, clearly keen to retaliate but lacking the physical or verbal skills required. 'I mean there for *me*. Just be nice. Be there if I ever want to talk or whatever.'

'What's the point?' his dad said, opening and closing his eyes like a rocked baby. 'You never say anything.'

'I want to though,' Greg said. 'I want to say plenty. I've got so many things I want to say that it feels like I'm going to explode if I don't. I'm not happy, Dad. I'm not happy and it's wrong and you should help. You should help me. I'd help you if you'd let me.'

'Sorry to disappoint you, but this is life, son,' his dad said almost in a whisper. 'Get used to it.'

'No,' Greg said, as his father gurgled and belched.

'What you want to be talking for anyway?' his dad asked, his neck slumped back to the angle which pointed towards the television. 'You a fairy like your brother?'

'If you say that again I will kill you,' Greg said quietly. 'I don't mean figuratively. I will end you right where you're sat and I'll do it with a smile.'

'Real men don't talk,' his dad mumbled. 'Real men get on with it. Your brother was a gobshite and look where that got him.'

'I wish you'd died instead of him,' Greg said, as his father's eyes closed once and for all, and for a moment he looked happy; satisfied to have finally reached oblivion. 'And I'll never forgive you for not feeling the same way.'

Suzanne could tell that Greg did not want to go home that day. It was a feeling she'd known all too well in the past. Nobody in the history of matrimony had been wed as long as she without facing periods where the most disheartening sight in the world is your own front door. Fortunately for Suzanne, and the man and the boys that she loved, she was nothing if not resilient. She'd ridden out her own difficulties with patience and overtime and for now, at least, she and her husband were as happy as they had ever been.

Whatever was keeping Greg from crossing his own threshold, she suspected it was more than just a rocky patch; and though the home was running unusually smoothly that day she couldn't bring herself to turf him out.

His Sunday shift had consisted of a six o'clock start, two bed baths, an hour in laundry, three changes of bedding, a full round of medication dispensary and a reorganisation of the pin-board to allow space for the Macmillan Coffee Morning posters and pamphlets left the day before.

'Come on,' Suzanne had said at ten past two. 'It's not the Sistine Chapel. You've more than earned your keep today, sunshine.'

Greg sighed and shrugged as she fussed needlessly around the reception desk.

'I'll just get it finished. There were a few dishes in the kitchen that wanted doing. I'll sort them out too.'

The dishes, Suzanne knew, had long since been cleaned and returned to their cupboards.

'Well, if you don't mind hanging around for a bit then there's some filing back here that needs doing. Stapling mostly, but you get to use the big stapler, so that's exciting I suppose?'

'Yeah,' Greg said, turning to face her.

'Yeah, son,' she said. 'Howay and let's make some use of you.'

'Cheers, Suzanne,' he said as she gave him a wink and began surreptitiously hunting for dummy paperwork she could keep him busy with, the way she'd find tasks for her own boys back when they were children just to keep them out of trouble.

'No bother, flower,' she said. 'I'm not paying you, mind,' she said and Greg laughed.

'Don't care really,' he said flatly. 'I've nothing to spend it on anyway.'

'Well if you're ever at a loose end my MOT wants doing and I prefer wine to chocolate. Either way, if you're going to be hanging around here for a bit you can make yourself useful. Come on – chop-chop. Get these files sorted,' she said and Greg nodded appreciatively.

'Do you want me to do you a coffee first?' he asked. Suzanne felt a small part of her heart break.

'You're the first man in a long time who's offered me a drink. I feel a bit overcome.'

'Steady on,' said Greg. 'We've only got instant.'

'At my age you take what you can get, my love. Go on, I'll take you up on the offer. Why don't you do yourself one an' all. I've ten minutes to spare. You and me can put our feet up, maybe have a little chat, eh?'

Greg nodded and made his way to the kitchens as Suzanne watched him go.

'Nectar, that,' Suzanne said, taking a sip of coffee as she sat at reception next to Greg. 'I might promote you to full-time barista.'

'I'm aiming for the top,' he deadpanned and she found herself reaching out and giving his back a small rub. There was, she knew, undoubtedly a rule somewhere against such physical affection between management and staff, but she could not bring herself to care. She wanted to take the boy and hug him tightly, promise blindly that things would one day be OK for him. The only thing that prevented her from doing just that was knowing it would render him mute with horror.

They were quiet for a while. Eventually Suzanne breathed in deeply.

'Everything OK then?' she asked, and Greg nodded. 'You feel like you're settling in a bit?'

'I like it,' he said. 'It's good.'

'Steady on. It's mopping shit and making tea on the whole, but it has its perks.'

'I live with my dad,' Greg said. 'At least here I'm getting paid for that.'

Suzanne laughed into her cup so hard that the coffee tickled her nose.

'Well, every cloud I suppose. How is Dad?' she said, and Greg shrugged. 'Everything OK at home?' she asked, and again he shrugged. 'You know . . .' she tried after another strained pause, uncertain as to whether she was reading the situation correctly. 'My sister died a good while ago,' she offered, and for the first time since she had known him Greg met her eyes with intent.

'Yeah,' he said, sipping his coffee even though it was still too hot. 'We should start a club.'

'She wasn't a bairn, not like . . .' she said, and stopped herself. 'Well, she wasn't a kid, that's all. But she was too young to go.'

'Were you close?' he asked and Suzanne nodded.

'Oh yeah,' she said. 'She was mine from day one. She was two years younger than me and the toughest person I ever knew. My little rock, our Viv. She was my bridesmaid and I was her

90

birthing partner for all three of her kids. Never went a day without talking.'

'I was close to Michael,' Greg said, staring at the floor again. 'He was two years younger, too. Probably would have been my bridesmaid if he'd ever had the chance,' he said and Suzanne laughed.

'When she passed,' she said, keen to stay strong for the boy but aware of just how deeply her own loss still cut her, 'it blew through me like a fucking hurricane. Nobody understood, you see. Nobody had lost what I had. We'd all suffered, granted. But grief, it's a different shape for everyone.'

'It's a different size, too,' Greg offered quietly, and she nodded.

Baxter made his way downstairs that day feeling spritely at the promise of a visit from an old friend. In the corridor he paused, suddenly aware of Greg and Suzanne deep in conversation. It was the first time he had heard the boy talk in this way and he was eager not to interrupt the moment lest he clam back up. Deep down, Baxter had hoped that Gregory would one day open up to him. He had never had a child of his own, but he'd always imagined his son or daughter would be a bit like Greg: that pig-headedness and pride, the bluff that he used to mask his deep need to be loved and comforted. Baxter had to admit he felt a little disappointed that Greg had not chosen him for a confidante; but he was pleased all the same that the boy had at least chosen someone.

'What I'm saying,' Suzanne went on, 'and I'm not clever like you, so maybe I'm not saying it right, is that ... people tell you it gets better, and you should listen to them.'

'Does it?' Greg asked hopefully.

'God, no. People are idiots,' Suzanne said. 'Don't know what they're on about. Just say what they think you want to hear. You should listen to them because they care, though, and knowing that people care makes a difference, whether you realise it or not.'

'So it'll always feel like this?' he asked, pleased for the honesty but wounded by the prospect of endless unhappiness.

'A bit. But it gets smaller,' she said, 'and further away. And before long it goes back to ... I don't know. It's like the hole they leave behind is smaller than the gap they filled when they were here. The happy outweighs the sad, eventually. You've just got to make sure you're strong enough to get to a point where that happens. Do you hear what I'm saying?'

Greg thought for a moment and nodded in agreement.

'Cheers, Suzanne,' he said as she tapped his knee firmly, just as the front doors shot open and a warm breeze blew in.

'Oh, look here,' she whispered from the corner of her mouth. 'Better get your chain and your knife, it's the Hell's Angels.'

Winnie rolled into Melrose Gardens at full speed on her new mobility scooter before drawing to a halt right at the reception desk.

'Hello, dear,' she said to Suzanne. 'I wanted a Porsche but my pension wouldn't stretch to it, you understand.'

'I know that feeling,' said Suzanne with a smile. 'How can I help you, flower?'

'I'm visiting a friend of mine,' said Winnie and then stopped dead, as Greg caught her eye.

'Gregory!' she hollered at the top of her voice. 'What an

absolute surprise and a delight! How are you, my dear?' she asked, clutching her hands to her heart with glee.

'All right, Miss,' Greg said with a smile. 'What you doing here?'

Winnifred – or Ms Milliner, to the children – had been the librarian at Gregory's school for nigh on three decades. She was a fond favourite of pupils through the years, but the teachers and management never quite got to grips with her renegade methods and values.

The school library doubled as a lending library for the surrounding community. Winnifred's rein had eventually come to an end when the service was faced with the threat of funding cuts and even potential closure. In response, Winnie had chained herself to the railings one morning before the start of her shift, and attracted the attention of two local newspapers, a camera crew, three firemen and the majority of the children. Dismissal seemed imminent, but Winnifred was nothing if not a fighter and – unfortunately for Headmaster Bishop, the governors, and the local council – she was also head of her workers' union. Thus she was promptly if grudgingly reallocated to a new role as head of reception where her main duties involved filing the morning registers and, unofficially, comforting pupils waiting outside the head's office with tales of her own youthful anarchy.

'Winnifred!' Baxter exclaimed, making his way around the corner.

'My prince!' she declared, embracing the old man.

'*Of course*,' Suzanne muttered, and Greg laughed, trying to piece together the two ill-fitting halves of his life.

'I thought you had a driving ban?'

'Long since expired, besides, the only danger I pose on this thing is death by starvation. It took me almost ten minutes to make it along from the high street. I'm a bundle of nerves.'

'Well if it's any consolation you look bloody ridiculous,' Baxter said as Winnie swatted at him.

'You're looking even more dapper than usual today, Mr Baxter,' Suzanne said, eyeing his rich navy suit jacket.

'A lily can grow even in a swamp,' he quipped back, still fascinated by the bodywork of Winnifred's new transportation. 'I take it you've been acquainted.'

'Oh yes,' said Winnifred. 'And you did not tell me you know *the* Greg Cullock!' she said. 'One of my favourites, young Gregory, though don't go spreading it else the others will get jealous.'

Baxter looked at Greg with surprise, only for the boy to shrug.

'You're not my only friend,' he said to the old man with a smirk. '*I know people.*'

'Evidently,' Baxter said with a chuckle.

'So what's the plan?' Winnie said. 'Are we staying here?'

'Not if you can't behave yourself,' Suzanne said.

'I make no promise,' said Baxter. 'Come, Winnifred! We shall take our luncheon in the public house.'

'You two watch how you go,' Suzanne said. 'I don't want to be getting calls to come and post bail at stupid o'clock in the morning.'

'Never!' cried Winnie. 'They'd have to catch us first.'

'And, Gregory,' added Baxter, 'if I'm not mistaken you're on an early shift today, no?'

'I said I'd help Suzanne with the filing,' Greg said.

'Then there is no question. You shall join us for lunch. My treat.'

'Oh yes!' said Winnie with her back to the room, struggling to locate the brake button. 'A lovely catch up, that's what we need, isn't that right, Gregory?'

'There goes my free labour,' Suzanne said, taking the filing from Greg's desk.

'Does that mean I can go then?' he asked and she nodded.

'You enjoy yourself, flower,' she said, as he made his way out from behind the desk. 'Just try not to let them lead you astray.'

10

The trio began with gin and tonics, before moving to beer and eventually settling on wine.

Two pints in on an empty stomach and Greg was relieved when Baxter and Winnie broke their impenetrable discourse to order lunch.

'Three roast beefs with extra Yorkshires and extra gravy.' Baxter logged the order as he made his way towards the bar.

Greg made a show of offering Baxter some cash for his share, and was relieved when his offer was declined.

'Your company, as always, Gregory, is payment enough. Just make sure Winnie doesn't talk to any questionable sorts when I'm gone.'

'So, my boy,' Winnie said, once Baxter was out of earshot. 'Are you well?'

'I suppose so, Miss,' he said with a half-hearted shrug.

'Please call me Winnie,' she said but Greg remained adamant.

'I'd sooner not if it's all the same,' he said apologetically. 'Doesn't seem right.'

'You do what feels right then, my love.'

'My leg's better,' he said with a smile. And, though it took the old woman a moment to get his reference, she eventually cottoned on.

'Very good,' she said, reaching out and placing her hand on his and giving it a comforting squeeze of surprising strength. 'What a lesson that is for us all. There is nothing we can break that can't be fixed, eh?'

'You're a very glass-half-full person,' Greg said, squeezing her hand in return as Winnie gulped the last three inches of her ale. 'For someone that drinks so quickly.'

'It's not a belief system,' she said. 'It's a tried and tested truth. Bar-room wisdom, my boy. Don't ever underestimate it.'

Ms Milliner insisted her title be pronounced with a Z sound on the end. It was the first time Greg had ever been introduced to a woman that was neither a Miss nor a Mrs, and the word took a while to settle in his mouth. More often than not he would revert back to the familiarity of 'Miss', as he did with all of his female teachers. And more often than not Ms Milliner would let it slide.

She was beloved by the students for a number of reasons. She had untamed hair and a ring on every finger. She had a gutsy, easy laugh and a kind smile that hid a wry sense of humour. Her language, when she thought she was alone, became gloriously coarse. And her contempt for the teachers she felt lacking was seldom hidden. Troubled students would seek her counsel, and a rumour started by Dean Fischer that he'd seen her drunk in an amusement arcade one Sunday afternoon only added to her appeal.

In Ms Milliner the children had an ally. Her loyalty was with the trickier students. She had time for anyone and everyone – no problem too trivial, no subject taboo – and she knew each by name.

In the weeks after his brother's death, Greg had found himself becoming better acquainted with the strange lady that guarded the reception desk.

'Sorry I'm late,' he'd mumble, turning up on Monday morning in Friday's uniform, twenty minutes after final bell and clearly unrested.

Her heart broke for the boy as it had broken for his brother. Michael had taken to Ms Milliner and would spend many an hour at her desk, making her laugh and listening to her stories. At least once a day the pair would talk until, one day, he stopped. He would pass her by without so much of a hello. Something, it seemed, had broken him. The light that shone inside of him had diminished and for over two weeks Ms Milliner watched the boy go through the motions, like a ghost left behind.

Then came the news.

'*Gregory*,' she had yelled, chirpily, on what was to be the first of many late mornings during those first few weeks. 'Come and say hello – you're already late, the damage is done.' And with leaden steps Greg approached her desk, and became another of the many students whose troubles were buffered by the guard of the old girl.

'I slept in,' he had offered, as she fussed with the returned registers and long-ignored paperwork that blanketed her desk.

'Do you know,' she told him, 'at my age I'd forget my head if it wasn't screwed on. I know I had a letter here somewhere from Mr Cullock about your emergency doctor's appointment this morning.'

'I never had a doctor's appointment ...' Greg mumbled, before being cut short by a raise of her hand.

'Absolutely terrible. Never get old, Gregory. First go the hips, then the mind. I just know I saw it somewhere. Your leg, per-haps, from all those sports you play? Do you think you could manage the odd limp for me over the next couple of days, and I'll have a word with Mr Bishop, informing him of my mistake with the note?'

Gregory blushed and nodded.

'Thanks, Miss,' he said. 'I reckon I can give it a go.'

'There's a lad,' she said, reaching out and tapping the boy's shoulder. 'Now, I take it you haven't had breakfast, what with the waiting times at the surgery. *Here*,' she said, passing over a loose handful of wrapped toffees, 'have these quickly in the toilets, that should keep you going until morning break. Now off you go, my love – there's learning to be done.'

After each variation on this conversational theme, she would watch as the boy treaded the linoleum towards another day of agony.

Baxter returned along with two willing members of the bar staff carrying a bottle of red, three empty glasses and a pot of horseradish for the table.

'It never fails to surprise me,' he said, edging into his seat carefully and letting his cane fall to the ground, 'just what a small world it is.'

'Me and Gregory go way back, isn't that right?' said Winnifred with a wink. Greg blushed.

'How do you two know each other?' Greg asked as Baxter slipped a five-pound note into the apron of the obliging staff who began to pour the wine.

'We were star-crossed from day one,' said Baxter, 'our lives interwoven from the off.'

'I used to run around his garden naked,' said Winnie, taking

100

a hearty glug of her wine, 'until the neighbours cut down their hedges.'

'Winnifred's sister was my oldest friend.'

'My darling Peggy,' said Winnie, raising her glass as Baxter joined her in the silent toast.

'And then, when she passed, Winnie was of age to take her place as my comrade in arms. We've had some good times, she and I.'

'I'll bet,' said Greg.

'I walked her down the aisle at all three of her weddings.'

'I never thought you were married,' Greg said.

'I wish I hadn't been,' she offered. 'Each one a disaster, but I got some lovely dresses out of them.'

Greg took a sip of his wine and forced himself not to grimace. It was a drink he was unfamiliar with; it tasted serious and knowing, like liquid talk radio. It was one he was not convinced he would be able to stick with, but with a cast-iron stomach and a desire for inebriation he persevered nonetheless.

'We all thought you were a lezza, Miss,' he said sheepishly as Winnie hooted with glee.

'Lezza . . .' Baxter whispered, toying with the word. '*How exotic.*'

'Oh, but I was!' she objected, clutching her hands to her chest. 'For twenty glorious minutes on a punt in Oxford. Sixty-two, I believe.'

'Lord, have mercy,' said Baxter, shaking his head.

'Guinevere Thompson. Oh, she was handsome,' Winnie went on. 'Hands like charger plates. Had the charisma of a young Iris Murdoch,' she said proudly, sipping her wine.

To prove her youthful beauty, Winnifred pulled a photograph from her purse and handed it to Greg as the heaving plates of beef and trimmings were laid out before them.

It showed her and Baxter wearing swimming costumes, laughing at a lost joke, the sea in the background flat and glistening even in black and white.

'I was quite the piece, eh?' she said, as Greg returned the photo.

'You were fit,' he conceded. 'You can tell you're old, though.'

Winnie let out a laugh.

'I beg your bloody pardon!' she said with mock indignation, thrilled by his candour. Greg was the type of boy that she loved the most. His were the jokes that never quite landed, the voice guaranteed to break during the presentation at work. He was a well-meaning fool, constantly apologising for his own failings. And no matter how old he got, there would always be a part of Greg that was a mortified little boy.

'Little shit!' Baxter yelled, slapping a napkin across the top of Greg's arm.

'I don't mean now!' he said. 'I just mean the photo, the way everything looks ... you can tell you're not a modern girl.'

'Say what you mean and there can be no misunderstandings,' Baxter said, drowning his meal in a sea of horseradish.

'Oh, Gregory,' said Winnie, placing her napkin on her lap, 'what a lot there is to teach you. As far as girls went I was the most modern of them all.'

'First person in our street to be fitted with a coil, isn't that right, Winnifred?' Baxter asked proudly, only to be met with an equally proud nod.

'Rusted within the fortnight,' she said to Greg with a cheeky raise of her eyebrows, causing the boy's face to burn scarlet.

'So you were never one of her husbands, then?' Greg asked, keen to change the subject.

Baxter and Winnie looked at one another before breaking into mutual hysterics.

'God knows I tried, Gregory,' said Winnie. 'God knows I tried. Alas, our love was to be chaste.'

'Well, we're still young,' Baxter offered with a wink and Winnie pretended to fan herself.

'That's not so say we weren't engaged, though,' she said knowingly.

'Time and time again.'

'The most promising young couple you ever did see!' Winnie said, clinking her glass against Baxter's.

Baxter and Winnie's friendship was born of loss and cemented in hedonism which took them both around the world twice over. Though both claimed ownership for the ingenious idea, neither could quite recall where the marriage scam began.

Perhaps it was Tangiers, where Winnie realised that she'd left her bag in the hotel bar and Baxter's wallet seemed to have disappeared from his jacket pocket. Maybe it was Paris, where their thirst for champagne was sharply challenged on seeing the price of a small glass, let alone a bottle. Either way, before long one or the other came up with their ruse, thanks to the well-worn ring box containing his mother's diamond band.

Baxter would get down on one knee, and stare up at Winnie, who'd fan herself and shriek her joy before accepting his proposal. The room around them would whoop and clap. Generous whispers were made into the ears of management and the rest of their night, more often than not, was complimentary.

Three cheers to young love!

Economy seats were upgraded to first class on aeroplanes; twin rooms became the finest suites at no extra charge; expensive bottles arrived at their dining tables out of the blue; and fancy desserts were delivered at the end of a thousand dinners, with their hosts' congratulations sung in every language you could name.

That small box, and their brazen audacity, had afforded them thousands in perks over the years. It was their proudest achievement, and one Baxter was sad to concede would probably never happen again.

After the death of her sister, Winnifred had taken ownership of the grocery.

With the money from the sale of her property she had been able to take a course at secretarial college, in a bid to tide herself over without having to hawk tinned carrots and greying meat. Her ultimate goal had been to write, though she had yet to commit pen to paper in any meaningful way. Even then, in her eightieth year, Baxter would rib her about it.

'And where is this novel of yours?' he'd ask, and she'd roll her eyes.

'There's no rush! One must live life before attempting to commit it to the page. I'm doing essential research here, old boy.'

Winnie was still certain that she'd one day make it as the *enfant terrible* of British letters.

Somewhere between sticky toffee pudding and bottle number two, Greg had slumped back in his seat and fallen asleep, mouth agape and body lumpen.

'The youth of today,' Baxter said, topping up Winnie's glass.

'No stamina,' she added, clinking her glass against his.

'You'd have liked his brother,' she said to Baxter, as the pair sat quietly, staring at the dozing boy. 'He was . . . what is it they say . . . *flamboyant*?'

'Bugger off,' said Baxter with a laugh, eyeing the barmaid for the bill. 'What exactly went on there?' he asked. 'He never talks about it, though God knows I've tried.'

And so Winnie relayed the story of Michael Cullock. She told him of the black eyes and the cruel whispers, the graffiti and the gangs and the chanting and the rumours and the helplessness she felt as she watched the boy be ground down to nothing.

'He hung himself in the end,' she said bluntly, unable to dilute the horror of his death. 'Walked out of school one day and took a rope into the woods. He was found by a dog walker, the way they usually are. The school did an assembly.'

Baxter felt his own insides tremble with a quiet fury at the boy's fate. He had fought hard for his own freedoms and had wanted to pass along a fairer world. For a while he thought that perhaps he had succeeded in his own small way; his refusal to hide in the face of prejudice was both personal and political, and he hoped he and others like him had made things easier for the next generation.

It was stories such as Michael's which made him realise how far was left to travel.

'I had no idea,' he said quietly, keen not to wake Greg. 'I thought it had changed. I thought you could be anything you wanted to be now.'

Winnie shook her head and wiped a tear from her eye. 'Not on the top deck of a school bus you can't.'

'It gets better, though,' Baxter said, as if as a question. 'Isn't that what they say?'

Winnie sighed and felt her voice weaken. 'One has to be able to see the light at the end of the tunnel if they are to make it out alive. Poor Michael was shut out before he had a chance to see just how close he was to making it.'

They sat for a moment, allowing the noise of the pub to wash over them as they toasted the lost boy.

'And what of this one?' asked Winnie eventually, nodding to Greg. 'I do worry, you know. I never thought I'd see him again.'

Baxter considered Gregory, who was now snoring into his chin, and shook his head.

'God only knows,' he said sadly. 'There's something there. But he's become so attached to it, the grief. He's tended to it like a garden and it's bloomed.'

'Sounds familiar,' Winnie said with a raise of her eyebrows, as Baxter swatted the suggestion away.

'Not like me,' he objected. 'I was never that young, for a start. But yes, it's as if he's given up. Still a child and already he's defeated.'

'I hope not,' said Winnie. 'He is such a good lad. Clever as anything and a hard little worker.'

'I know,' said Baxter. 'He's not as dumb as he looks. Or acts. He's certainly a pain, and mouthy in all the wrong ways but he's a good heart. Hopefully that will carry him through. I only wish I'd met him long ago. I'm not sure I've the energy to pull him out of whatever mire he's gotten himself into, at my stage in life. Something about him makes me want to try, though.'

'That you try will make a difference,' Winnie said, 'whether you realise it or not.'

'I just wish someone would light a bloody fire under him – remind him that the world won't come to meet him, he must rise to meet *it*.'

'He's been hurt, Baxter,' Winnie said. 'You of all people should be able to see that. He's been wounded in a way that can never fully heal.'

'So has everyone, at one point or another.'

'Not so young, though, you said so yourself, and not so horribly. He's just doing what he can to survive.'

'But I don't just want him to survive,' Baxter said. 'I want him to *live*. I won't be around much longer to help him, but I must ensure he's left in a position where he is able to help himself. To allow Gregory to disappear would be a great disservice to the world, and I am not going to sit back and watch it happen.'

Winnie shook her head and stretched out her hand for Baxter's.

'You can't save them all, Mr Baxter,' she whispered, as the old man wiped a rogue tear from behind the rim of his glasses.

'No,' he said, looking down at the boy. 'No,' he said again. 'But they must know that we tried. To simply stop feeling is no way to avoid pain.'

'He'll come right,' said Winnie.

'Once you stop giving a damn it's very difficult to start again. I just want to know that he cares, that's all. About something. About anything. Then I'll be happy.'

Winnie smiled. 'You'll never be happy, Baxter. You and I shall live to a hundred as the world's most miserable sods and then die unsatisfied. It's written in the stars.' She winked and sipped her wine as Baxter laughed.

'What else?' she said after a while. 'I can tell something's up.' She nudged his ankle with her foot.

Baxter breathed heavily and was grateful that with Winnie there were certain blanks he would never have to fill in.

'I can't go without saying goodbye to Thomas,' he said eventually. 'I just can't leave him all the way over there without ...' he said, and then stopped himself as Winnie gripped his hand tightly. 'He can't just disappear with me. All those days. All that love.'

'I know,' she said, 'I know. You must do what you must do.'

'Am I a stupid old man?' he asked and she laughed, reaching to wipe another tear from his eye.

'Yes, of course,' she said, her own voice wavering with emotion. 'The stupidest there ever was probably. But a good one, and that's what counts. If you cannot rest until you've said goodbye, then there is only one thing for it.'

'There are more practical matters to deal with, of course,' Baxter went on, polishing his glasses on the cuff of his shirt. 'I would like to begin proceedings to have him named. His grave should not be blank – he should be honoured. Invisibility is not right. None of it is right.'

'I'll say,' said Winnie.

'Will you help me?' Baxter asked. 'Find out whom I must contact to set things in motion? Perhaps even write a letter? I've left it so late,' he said, 'and now all my tomorrows have come at once, and I'm not entirely sure I'm able to process them in time.'

'Of course I can,' Winnie said, touched that the old man had asked for help for the first time in his life.

'Good,' he said, finishing his wine. 'You always were my favourite writer.'

'Aha,' said Winnie, 'but you never saw any of my work.'

'Call it a hunch,' he said, draining his glass as the old woman smiled and then laughed.

'Oh, Baxter, I do love you,' she said warmly.

'And I you, Milliner,' he replied with a wink.

108

11

Baxter had slept through both breakfast and morning coffee, and had taken to obscenities when a member of the temp staff came to check on him shortly after ten. He made his way to the small desk in his bedroom. Alcohol emanated from his skin like heat from a runway on touchdown. And though he hadn't smoked in many years his chest felt as though it had been sat on by one of the home's heavier occupants.

'Can't handle it like you used to, old boy,' he said with a croaking voice.

He propped his iPad against the record player and opened the web page he had found between naps. From his top drawer he removed a pad of paper, a bound stack of envelopes and a book of stamps along with his favourite ballpoint.

His time with Winnifred had fortified him as it always did. Something about the woman made him feel so young and their conversation about Thomas had cemented and clarified his mission: he was determined to pay his respects before it was too late.

He took up his pen and set to work.

Dear Sir or Madam, he began, and immediately he felt a rush of shame as though he'd made a mistake in front of the entire class.

'Nonsense,' he muttered to himself, balling the paper and tossing it dramatically over his shoulder so that it sprung off the wall and landed on his bedspread. 'Tell me what to say, old boy,' he muttered. 'You were always so good at introductions.'

He tried again.

To whom it may concern,

He sat back, considered a while, decided it would do.

I am seeking information on how to secure acknowledgement of a previously unnamed soldier, missing presumed dead since the Second World War.

I am ninety-four years old and not exactly in rude health. In fact I am hurtling at breakneck speed towards finality, and so would appreciate a swift response as to the correct course of action, by post to the below address, at your earliest convenience.

I thank you in advance for your time and advice.

Baxter stared down at the words momentarily, considered them line by line. His head still throbbed but he felt fractionally better for having accomplished his task.

He folded the letter and sealed it inside the envelope, adding two stamps to be safe. Squinting at the iPad, he carefully wrote out the address suggested online.

'Bugger,' he said, checking his watch and realising it was barely ten minutes before last post.

A spritelier man could make it, but if he tried in his current state he'd end up sprawled on a pavement awaiting an ambulance. So, despite repeated warnings from Suzanne, he pressed the alarm button usually reserved for falls, and sat back, awaiting his unwitting courier.

Ramila sat in the conservatory observing the quiet hum of life around her as outside it started to rain.

Dot Ballard played dominos at a small table in the centre of the room, her opponent invisible in the chair opposite, which she would pull out each morning out of habit and sentiment.

A group of the old girls had formed a makeshift knitting circle along the sofas.

'Mine's a gin and tonic,' Elsie said to Ramila, tapping her shoulder with a knitting needle as she went to join them.

Ramila watched as Elsie planted herself down next to Mary and wiggled herself against her to clear a space.

'She's making my hip bad,' Mary complained.

'If she did her exercises more she'd be fine,' Elsie objected to the hushed tittering of the ladies either side of the pair.

'Don't make me come over there, girls,' Ramila said. 'I'll not think twice about clothes-lining the lot of you.'

The ladies simmered to silence and carried on with their shared task.

'You can do anything you like to me,' said Ivan in a filthy growl, as he picked up a watering can and started wetting an aspidistra, much to the fury of Morris Boyle, who had long considered himself to be the home's premier indoor gardener.

Ramila raised her eyes slowly and glared at her admirer.

'Careful what you wish for,' she said slowly, for Ivan posed no real threat. 'Us girls have learned a thing or two since you were playing to win. I could break you in half bonnie lad, make no mistakes,' she continued, as Ivan's eyes widened and he shuffled

111

off to dampen the earth of a cheese plant whose leaves had begun to curl.

'OK, guys,' she said to the room at large. 'Team chat. This is serious, too, OK, so I need you to get your heads in the game here. Twelve across. Nine letters. 1945 love story. *Brief* something. There's a T and an R in the mix, if that helps,' she said, to stony silence. 'Come on! If I get this I can enter to win two hundred and fifty quid. I'll buy you a box of biscuits.' It was no use. 'Whatever. You're all dead to me,' she muttered, flicking the page.

'It's "Encounter",' Baxter said, entering the conservatory and taking a seat next to Ramila. *'Brief Encounter.* It's a film. Came out the year the war ended.'

Ramila flicked back her page and checked that the answer fit.

'You little bloody smasher,' she said as Baxter nodded in agreement.

'Caught it on a double bill at the Odeon in town. Bawled my eyes out and let me tell you, back in those days that got you looks.'

Ramila tapped Baxter's knee and turned to face him, returning her magazine to the side table.

'You old romantic,' she said, gently kneeing his thigh. Baxter shrugged. 'Sad ending, was it?' she asked and Baxter nodded.

'No love story can ever have a happy ending, if you think about it.'

Ramila considered this and nodded.

'I suppose you're right,' she conceded. 'bleak as fuck, mind.'

Nodding towards the knitting circle, Ramila said, 'You after some new gear, Baxter?'

Baxter scoffed. 'How about a rose from your suitor?' he said, eyeing Ivan. 'At your age you can't be too picky. Give the old boy a chance,' he said through a smirk.

'Very bloody funny,' she hissed, passing him an open packet of biscuits from which he took two crumbling garibaldis. 'I'm practically a child. There are Disney stars older than me, thank you very much. I still get asked for ID in nightclubs.'

Baxter nodded as he ate.

'And what of Mrs Ballard?' he asked. 'Is she expecting a visitor, or does she just prefer to know she'll win.'

'Dottie?' Ramila said. 'She's playing for Bill.'

'There's a Mr Ballard?' he asked, surprised that he was yet to be acquainted with her other half.

'Was. He went just before you got here. Bill was lush. Proper old charmer. Used to bring us biscuits back when he'd been into town and everything. He did all sorts for her.'

Baxter felt a familiar sadness as he remembered those first days when he went from 'we' back to 'I'. The cruelty of a half full frying pan, or a bed with room to sprawl.

'They would play together every day,' Ramila said. 'It was so cute. She'd set up the game and he'd come in with two coffees. They never said anything, either. Don't suppose there's anything left to say by the time you get to their age. They'd just do this thing together that they both loved, then they'd pack up their game and go up for a nap.'

'And she can't bear to let go of the routine,' said Baxter.

'It's as if she thinks if she keeps doing it he might come back one day,' she said. 'Or she'll never forget him. She's not well. Her memory is going and it's taking Bill with it. It's awful really, I've seen it before. Not so much when it's gone completely, but

113

when it's there just enough for you know it's slipping away, that's when it really gets you.'

'How heartbreaking,' Baxter said, remembering his own futile routines during the time before he realised his circumstances were to be unchanging. The extra place set for dinner, or the second glass poured without thinking. He still did not know whether such instances of mild insanity were merely a force of habit, or a desperate attempt to alter time's arrow, but he knew how poignant those moments had been, and how in their own small way they had helped him to cope.

'And yet how lovely, to have known love so deeply that you can never quite accept life without it,' he added.

'So sweet, isn't it?' Ramila said. 'She's to be watched, though, is Dottie. Had a fall the other week and went at Suzanne with a nail file when she tried to have a look at the graze on her head. Almost had her eye out.'

'One does what one must do to survive,' Baxter said with a smile, pleased to hear that whatever faculties were leaving her, the old girl still had some fight left.

'I'll say,' Ramila added as Baxter made his way from his chair. 'Oh, you off then?'

'The day must be faced head on,' he said. 'I shall take a trip to the high street. Would you like to accompany me?'

Ramila grudgingly shook her head.

'Suzanne would go spare,' she said. 'Already on the warpath at how pissed you got our Greg last night,' she said and Baxter laughed.

'The body of an ox and the constitution of a mouse. Anyway, how does she know?'

Ramila smiled and took her phone from its hiding place in her headscarf.

'Got this at teatime,' she said to Baxter, showing him a message comprising mostly of consonants. 'I was bad laughing at it, bless him.'

'Oh good, so that's another conversation I have to look forward to.'

'What a time to be alive,' Ramila deadpanned and Baxter nodded as he made his way from the door. 'If you are nipping over the road, though,' she added, with a keen look in her eye, 'pick me up a Greggs on the way back. Nothing much, just a tuna crunch baguette and a cheese and bean melt, yeah?'

'Anything else?'

'An iced split and a Capri Sun if you can manage it? I'll give you the cash on payday.'

'Your wish, my dear, is my command.'

'What did I say to you?' Suzanne yelled as Greg made his way into Melrose Gardens, twenty minutes late for his shift and looking like death.

He mumbled an apology but couldn't quite bring himself to meet her eye. His stomach gurgled with the ache of yesterday's wine, causing his entire body to tremble like a leaf.

'I said . . .' she went on, taking in the sight of the boy. She was pleased, in her own small way, that he had clearly enjoyed the night. But not enough to let her righteous fury dim completely. '. . . I told you they'd have you bad within the hour, and what happens?'

'I think I ate some bad beef,' Greg tried in vain.

'I think you drank some shitty wine,' she said. 'And God knows how many pints. Had to pour bloody Winnie into a taxi when she got back here. Look at the state of the desk,' she said, pointing towards a scuffed dent at the base of her throne. 'She came at reception on that scooter like a fucking missile. I thought she'd gone over the handlebars at first, stupid old woman.'

Greg smirked at the thought of Winnie crashing into Melrose Gardens at full speed, though was quick to extinguish his joy as Suzanne arched an eyebrow.

Baxter stood outside the retirement home, watching a scowling Suzanne and a godforsaken Greg. He had to brave it. He picked up his pace and scuttled past the desk as fast as his bones would let him.

'Good afternoon,' he said, without pause for response.

'Oi!' Suzanne yelled as Baxter made his way around the corner towards the lifts. 'I want a word with you.'

'It will have to wait,' he said, in no way slowing his progress. 'I am quite harrowed by the high streets. I shall take to my bed for the rest of the afternoon. Gregory, a hand if you will.'

'Don't you bloody move,' Suzanne warned the boy. 'Get here now!' she tried again, though Baxter was already out of sight.

'Gregory,' Baxter hollered, as he frantically pushed the button for the lift. 'A hand?'

The boy looked at his manager, who shook her head and sighed.

'Go on then,' she said grudgingly. 'Bugger off and see what he wants. Mind, I want you back down here within ten minutes, there's real work to be done.

'And if that emergency cord gets pulled again and you're not on death's door you'll know about it all right,' Suzanne yelled at Baxter as the lift doors shut.

*

Greg made his way into the bedroom and slumped into Baxter's chair.

'Aren't you feeling rough?' he asked the old man, who placed his bag of toiletries in his top drawer and took a seat on the bed.

'Absolutely not. Right as rain. Was up with the larks as per usual,' he lied, rubbing his glasses on the sleeve of his shirt. 'Hand me that machine, will you?' Baxter said, pointing at the iPad as Greg slowly obliged, still uncertain as to whether he could survive a day's work.

'Your company was appreciated,' Baxter said, scanning through files on his tablet. 'Winnifred was happy to see you.'

Greg smiled and shrugged.

'Same. I never thought I'd see her again. And it was nice seeing the two of you together,' Greg said to Baxter's surprise.

'Really? Most people find us impenetrable show-offs.'

'You can tell you've been friends a long time.'

'Too bloody long,' Baxter muttered as he located what he was looking for on the iPad.

'It was the first night out I've had in ... well, ever,' Greg said, and Baxter looked up.

'Hardly a night,' he said with a smile. 'You barely made it to five o'clock.'

'You know what I mean,' Greg said. 'I had a good time. I'm not really used to that.'

'There shall be many more,' Baxter said, though Greg looked uncertain.

'Doubt it. I haven't really got any friends.'

Baxter cleared his throat and put his iPad to one side.

'Well, you have at least two now,' he said kindly, though he

117

knew it was little consolation. 'And the first few are the hardest. You've just got to remain open to the possibility.'

'Here's to hoping,' Greg said, before thanking Baxter. 'I really did enjoy it. I know it was just a couple of drinks and a meal, but . . .' he trailed off.

Baxter sighed and turned to the crumpled young man.

'I'm very fond of you, Gregory, do you know that?'

The boy shrugged with discomfort.

'*No*,' Baxter demanded. 'Don't look away. And don't bloody shrug, either. It's entirely unbecoming. What I want you to know is that I care about you, for what it's worth. I see in you parts of myself, and I see qualities I wish I'd had at your age, too. You're brave. You're kind. And no matter how hard you try to mask it, you're good at heart. If I can see it then so can the rest of the world. So buck up and get yourself out there, do you hear me?'

Greg nodded, trying not to blush.

'Tell me, Gregory,' he said, though he knew what the answer would be before he'd even posed the question. 'Is this where you want to be in life?'

Greg chuckled and shook his head.

'No, but it's where I am. Just got to get on with it,' he said.

'Bullshit,' said Baxter loudly, causing Greg to flinch. 'Absolute and utter nonsense. Now, sit up straight and talk to me like an adult, not some petulant child. Are you *happy*?'

'Is anyone?' Greg asked warily, correcting his posture at the old man's insistence.

'So help me God, my boy, I will get up and go at you with my walking stick if you're not careful,' Baxter warned. 'Sod everyone else. Bugger the world and its complacency, it can sort

118

itself out. I'm asking about *you*. Are *you* confident that this is to be your life?' he asked, leaning forwards. 'Are *you* happy? I want you to answer the question I asked.'

Greg thought for a moment and shook his head. 'No.'

'Good,' Baxter said, finally satisfied. 'Very good.'

'I'm pleased you're so happy about it.'

'Don't be obtuse. Your unhappiness brings me no joy, but your willingness to acknowledge it bodes well. It means you can change your course.'

'My ship's sailed,' Greg said flatly.

'You're eighteen years old,' said Baxter with an exhausted smile. 'Your ship hasn't even been built yet. Now enough of this silliness. What do you want to do?'

Greg shrugged.

'What do you want to *be*?'

Greg paused.

'Happy,' he said, almost apologetically.

'And is your happiness to be found in this current role?' Baxter asked, and Greg shook his head. 'Then let's do something about it, eh? I take it you would not be heartbroken to sacrifice your position?'

Greg shrugged. 'What did you have in mind?'

'Oh, nothing long-term,' Baxter said. 'That's on you. But I have an errand to run. An elaborate one and there's not much time. Tell me, have you ever been abroad?'

'No, never had the money,' Greg said, 'and Dad gets a rash if he has to drive any further than Durham. Why?' he asked. 'Is it any good?'

'You'll never know if you don't try,' Baxter said. 'I've to go to France, for this errand of mine.'

'You doing the booze cruise?' Greg asked and the old man laughed.

'If I were, you would not be my first choice of companion given last night's showing. No, no. Just a trip to see an old friend of mine, but of course I shall require assistance with the pragmatics of the journey. I've a spare ticket and would happily put your name to it,' he offered, though in truth the deed had already been done. 'If you'd be willing, then these are the dates and the times,' he said, scribbling onto a sheet of paper.

Greg stared at the information. 'Why me?'

'Because I care about you,' Baxter said. 'I see you, Gregory, and I see through you. You mistake stupidity for stoicism. You assume your silence is noble but it's not. It's toxic and corrosive. One cannot hide in the dark and expect to grow like the rest.'

'You seem pretty certain,' Greg said defensively.

'I am,' Baxter said. 'And that's because when I look at you I see myself.'

'Is that a good thing?' he asked, fidgeting in his seat.

'It could be, if you listen. I learned how to cope the hard way so you'd do very well to heed my advice and to trust me. Might save you the odd stumble,' Baxter said. 'Now, France. What about it? Do you good, I reckon. They say a change is as good as a rest, and you've certainly had long enough to rest. It's time to see what else there is. Besides,' he added, 'friends are hard to come by as well you know, harder still at my age. I'd far sooner go with a fond acquaintance than some hired hand to keep me from keeling over.'

'I can't stop you from dying,' Greg said.

'Nor do I expect you to. And nor do I expect you to answer right away. Just promise me you'll consider it. The fare is taken care of and the arrangements are in place. All I want to know is that you're open to the possibility.'

Greg hesitated for a moment.

'OK,' he said eventually. 'I'll think about it,' he added, slipping the details into the pocket of his uniform. 'It's not a no but it's not a yes.'

Baxter nodded.

'Baby steps,' Baxter said with a smile. 'Now bugger off and see what Suzanne wants. I must take my nap in peace. Today has been most taxing.'

He closed his eyes as the boy made his way from his bedroom, shutting the door behind him.

12

A clear sky and a warm breeze woke Baxter the next morning. It beckoned him towards the small garden immediately after breakfast, where already tables had been erected by Suzanne in anticipation of the summer rush.

Morris stood against the wall, guarding a small tap, keen not to let Ivan usurp him of his duties once more.

Ida Edmonds sat in the farthest corner, her wheelchair angled towards a bench where a speech therapist sat, her mouth making the shapes that her throat could not yet muster.

'Bit of Vitamin D, ladies, that'll sort you out,' said Suzanne, doling out choc-ices to the sweltering gals able to manage them. 'Come on, don't be shy. You've all got fine figures, a little treat to cool you down with won't hurt. Give it five minutes and I'll send Ramila out with the big brolly for a bit of shade.' June's red face and wilting frame *were* a little concerning. 'Here you are, pet,' Suzanne said, carefully removing the hat from Louis's head while he dozed in the shade, oblivious, and plonking it onto June's purple rinse. 'That'll do you for now.'

'Oh, Suzanne,' Baxter said sleepily. 'I was so relaxed in the glorious sunshine that I didn't even notice you were here.'

'I'm bloody sure,' she said, claiming a seat next to his and taking a moment to unwind, already five hours into her shift.

'My blood sugars feel adequately steadfast today,' he said, hungrily eying the box in her hands as she took an ice cream for herself.

'Oh aye,' she said, 'no funny turns this time?'

'Fit as a fiddle,' Baxter said, almost salivating at the thought of the sweet vanilla. 'If anything I think they might be low.'

'Hmmm,' Suzanne said, biting through chocolate. 'Clearly the moderation is doing you the world of good.'

'Clearly,' Baxter said through pursed lips and flared nostrils.

'Well,' she said, enjoying having the upper hand, 'just make sure you keep up with your five a day and cut back on puddings and we'll have you where you want to be in no time. That's a Melrose Gardens promise.'

Baxter sighed and tutted.

'Oh, that's just bloody charming, isn't it?' he grumbled as Suzanne began to laugh. 'I suppose this is punishment for Lord only knows what.'

'Take your pick, old boy,' she said, elaborately tucking into the last inch of her bar, which had begun to melt down her wrist.

'I shall report you to whichever authority will listen,' he said.

'Oh settle down, you old sod,' she said, passing him the last ice cream from the box. 'I'm only kidding. Like I'd leave you out, my darling.'

Baxter shook his head as he unwrapped his ice cream.

'Your kindness knows no bounds,' he said.

'You're telling me,' Suzanne added, sitting up to face Baxter as the old man made his way through the ice cream in four glorious mouthfuls.

'There,' she said, as he handed her the wrapper, 'that's put a smile on your face, eh?'

Baxter nodded and shook his head in one uncertain movement.

'Only insomuch as I don't like to trouble you, my dear,' he said. 'You'll get your reward in heaven.'

'I'll get my reward come performance review, which is today, in case you were wondering.'

'Ah,' said Baxter, removing his glasses perkily. 'A visit from the top?'

'Mr Patel will be touring the facility today, yes,' she sighed.

'And no doubt he'll want some feedback from his most recent and compos mentis residents,' Baxter said with a wink.

'I daresay. But rest assured, sunshine – this review is the only thing separating me from a fortnight in Lanzarote come October,' she said. 'So don't think for one moment I'm above slipping a fistful of downers into your morning coffee.'

Baxter laughed. In truth he could think of few who deserved a raise more than Suzanne.

'And what's in it for me?'

'Oh,' she said, leaning back in her chair. 'Just you wait. I can make life very difficult for you, Mr B.' She slapped his leg playfully as together they took in the sun.

'Yes,' he said, tapping her leg in return. 'You've demonstrated as much almost constantly since my arrival.'

'You ain't seen nothing yet,' she said, as a small patch of cloud passed over the sun, momentarily cooling the yard around them.

'In all seriousness,' Baxter said, after a moment's silence, 'I did want to speak with you.'

'Oh aye,' Suzanne said, sitting up and readying herself to take to her swollen feet once more. 'That sounds ominous. Come on then, out with it.'

Baxter smiled and shrugged his shoulders. There was no way, sitting there in the walled yard of a backstreet nursing home, beside a woman he had known for less than a month, he could begin to explain the great urgency, the mixture of love and loss and time that was pulling him to go.

'I must go to France,' he said with certainty. 'The importance of the task I cannot put into words, and that's a fresh sensation for me, let me tell you.'

'Oh, love . . .' She felt for the man. 'Look—'

'No, you look,' he interrupted sharply. 'The wheels are in motion and the fact is I'm going. I've acquired tickets, arranged accommodation and attained a charming selection of travel-sized toiletries to see me through. I have made arrangements and that is that.'

'Have you indeed?' she asked, as the old man simmered down.

'Indeed I have. A pot of pomade no bigger than a Pontefract cake. Would you believe it? What a time to be alive!'

'It's the keeping you alive that I'm bothered about,' she said. 'We've been through this, flower. You know as well as I do that it's not something I can sign off on. That's just how it goes.'

'Suzanne, I ask out of common courtesy,' he said as she rolled her eyes at him, 'but you must know how important this is to me and I *am* going. Have you ever cared about something so much that your own welfare ceases to matter? One day I may well tell you the story from the beginning but until then, just know that I'll not rest peacefully unless I have done what I need to do. I *need* to go, Suzanne.'

126

Suzanne shook her head, plucking a cigarette stub from the earth between two paving stones, and slipping it into the empty box she carried under her arm. She could not personally, morally, professionally or otherwise, be seen as endorsing his mission. That's just how it went.

The paperwork alone would bury her for weeks. Not to mention the personal anguish she'd feel. She'd not slept for three nights running when the knitting circle missed their coach back from a tour of Bury Market and Morecambe Bay, thanks to Violet's tricky hip and a lengthy queue at the gift shop.

France would send her to an early grave, whether or not Baxter survived the journey, of that she was certain.

And yet in his eyes she could see the hurt; see the desperation of an unlikely voyage becoming less likely by the day.

She could not be the one to sanction it, but nor could she be the one to stop it completely.

'Baxter,' she tried. 'You're an intelligent man,' she said and he nodded, making her want to slap him across the head for his gross overconfidence. 'So listen to me and listen carefully. Despite your best efforts, nothing you can do would cause me more bloody grief than buggering off on some last-minute jaunt in your current state.'

Baxter's heart sank.

'But,' she went on, 'you're a bookish sort, as you're so bloody well keen to remind everybody, so read between the lines here. As your friend, I've asked you not to pursue your little mission. As your professional carer, I've categorically said no. And I will record both of these facts to cover my back. But that's as far as I'm willing to fight you on this one. I mean it when I say no, but even my authority has its limits, believe it or not. So you just have a good long think about what's important, and you act accordingly. *All right?*' she said, wary at her loose concession and still hoping, deep down, that the old man would relent.

Baxter smiled and reached out to take her hand in his.

'You're a good woman, Suzanne,' he said, and she nodded in agreement.

'They broke the mould, let me tell you.'

Baxter nodded and smiled, removing his hand from hers and returning his sunglasses to his eyes as he sat back down in his chair.

'You'll have Lanzarote come October, my girl,' he said, as she made her way back inside. 'One way or the other, I shall see that it's done.'

Suzanne shifted in her seat as her meeting with Mr Patel drew to its conclusion.

She had never been a frivolous woman. Even as a girl her head had been firmly on her shoulders. She had taken a job at the earliest opportunity and worked her way up through the ranks. She had married the first man that had asked, and slid seamlessly from being a good daughter to a good wife and ultimately a good mother without so much as pausing once to consider where she fitted into the arrangement.

It was because of this lifelong diligence that she allowed herself a moment of silliness when faced with her boss. For since the day she had sat in that very office, gripping a crisp copy of her CV and sweating through the fabric of her finest blouse, she'd had a crush on him. A silly word for a silly notion but there was no other term for it. She knew that the situation would never develop. She'd run a mile before considering anything as reckless as an affair. But she did not chastise herself for her girlish affection. She felt about him the way she felt about holiday programmes and non-sale items in department stores. The fun was in theory only. She would allow herself to look, and would go no further.

'So that's that then,' he said, wrapping up their meeting. 'Oh,' he said, raising his finger just as Suzanne was standing up, causing her to sink back gladly into the comfy seat with the perfect view. 'The new resident. Mr . . .'

'Baxter,' she said flatly, forcing a smile.

'Quite the troublesome character on arrival,' Mr Patel chuckled.

'He's a card,' she said, as close to nonchalant as she could manage.

'During his first two days I had three emails, two phone calls to my private number and a house visit from a policeman with regards to allegations of forced imprisonment.'

The room was silent as Suzanne tried to justify the old man's actions.

'What's he like, eh?' she said eventually.

'You tell me. I take it he has since settled in.'

'Oh yes,' Suzanne said, standing up once more. 'We're like family now. Can't get enough of the place. He's a lovely old boy once you get to know him.'

'So it's a good fit, you'd say?' he asked and Suzanne forced the most convincing smile she could muster.

'He's having a smashing time,' she said, collecting the coffee cups. 'And we're all just so glad we're getting to know him.'

'Very good.' Mr Patel nodded.

'Oh yes,' said Suzanne, making her way to the door. 'A real corker, our Baxter. One in a million. Every moment a gift.'

*

Winnifred woke late that morning, surrounded by books.

Baxter had been gone for weeks now and she found she was lonely for the first time in eight decades.

She slept till late each morning and spent her first waking hours in bed with a slice of cake and her laptop for company, perusing the news and ordering frivolities.

At sundown she'd pour herself a gin. There would be wine with dinner in front of the television, after which she would put on her music and reach for her books.

She loved fiction most of all but occasionally she wanted nothing more than to read poetry for an entire evening. Her whole body would move to its rhythm as though she had spent the day at sea. It felt both nourishing and necessary. In poems, she found strength. She knew she could keep going.

Closing the window of her Twitter account, she readied herself to rise and greet the day ahead.

'Oh hello,' she said to nobody in particular, as her email pinged once with a new message. She smiled when she saw the sender's name.

Good morning, my dear.

I hope you are well. I elected not to phone, as I can never be certain of the hours you keep. Suffice to say that the wheels are in motion and the game is afoot.

Ergo: I am off!

With love and best wishes

Your prince

Baxter

X

13

Greg lay in bed that morning, sweat-drenched.

The sun hung low and heavy, and his room was sealed in its own warmth. With hot hands he pushed his damp fringe from his eyes. It seemed to hold fast in its own oils.

His uniform lay washed, ironed and draped over the radiator where he had placed it the evening before. He had cleaned and hoovered his bedroom after the previous day's shift, the stray beer cans and crisp packets stacked, bagged, hauled downstairs and thrust into the already heaving recycling bin.

He had changed his bedding and sprayed scent from a plastic bottle across his curtains and rug. He had bleached his skirting boards and cleared his mantelpiece.

The only object not binned or hidden from view was the scrap of paper Baxter had given him with the details of tomorrow's journey scribbled in the old man's exquisite copperplate. He had placed it beneath a water glass on the windowsill.

'You not at work today then?' Teddy asked, dumping one box of tools on the kitchen table and retrieving another from the cupboard.

Greg placed two slices of bread on the grill and turned to his father.

'Do you want me to make you some? It'll not take long,' he asked.

'Some of us haven't got time for elevenses,' Teddy said, nodding at the clock.

'It's my day off,' Greg said, sliding the tray beneath the flame of the grill. 'I thought I might clear out the garden.'

His dad looked out through the kitchen window into the decaying tangle of their small back yard.

'What do you want to do that for?' he asked. 'It's a shit-heap out there.'

Greg shrugged, grabbing a tea towel in anticipation of the smoke alarm.

'Something to do, isn't it?' he said. 'It might be nice. If it's still warm we could sit outside on an evening. Get some air. We could even have our tea out there. I might get a little table and some plants and stuff come payday. What do you think?'

Teddy stared at his son.

'So you want to be a gardener now?' he asked doubtfully. 'Is that it?'

Greg sighed and breathed in deeply, counting to ten in his head. Unusually he was reluctant to begin a fight with his father.

'I just thought it would be nice,' he said. 'Nice to do. Nice to have. Something different. A bit of a change.'

Teddy thought for a moment.

'Whatever you like,' he said, heading for the door. 'Just don't touch anything in my shed. Cost a bloody fortune and I don't want you messing it up.'

As he walked away, the kitchen filled with the dark scent of burning bread.

Greg's enthusiasm waned within moments of embarking upon his task.

The yard was small but cluttered. Weeds grew strong from cracks in the paving slabs. Snails swarmed across the stone patio, punctuating his progress with intermittent crunch and squelch.

Heeding his father's warning not to touch his tools, he had improvised as best he could with household goods. His armoury was laid out along the back step. For his excavation he had amassed a butter knife, the good kitchen scissors, a bottle of thick bleach, a screwdriver that he'd found on top of the electric meter, a whole roll of unopened bin liners, two cans of cherry Coke and a broom with a broken handle.

His phone was set to his preferred radio station and he had secured a pair of Marigolds which he wore for protection, along with a pair of his father's old jogging bottoms and a T-shirt with a hole in whose origin he could not recall.

The trickiest of his tasks, though by no means the hardest, was deciding where to start. The mess was so established that it seemed to have developed its own order. He knew, rationally, that no amount of effort would result in the miniature oasis that he had initially envisioned. It would be the same shithole yard. Just tidier.

He gripped his butter knife in one hand, breathed in deeply and looked around, contemplating his first move carefully before bending down and immediately cultivating the first of many nettle stings that day.

'Fuck's sake,' he said.

Before long it became second nature. For all his aching muscles and growing array of stings and cuts, the repetition was meditative. Patch by patch he'd clear the path with the most appropriate tool for the job. He would pull up weeds from their roots and slip them into bin bags which he'd take out to the back lane.

He forced himself to focus. It was slow progress to start with but after a while, and to his delight, the fruits of his efforts became apparent. Slowly the yard began to resemble a space safe for human occupation. A space one might even enjoy spending time in.

The stings across his fingers and arms brought back memories of the days he and Michael would spend together deep in the woods, raking out leaves and branches to create the perfect den or fortress, depending on their mood.

'Can we make a separate room for snacks?' Michael would ask, kicking twigs out of the way whilst Greg created the skeleton of their makeshift digs.

'You can give me a hand, how about that?' he'd snap, overheated from effort and tired before their fort had even taken shape.

Michael, though far from athletic, was fearless and lithe. He would spend most of the time climbing trees, swinging upside down from branches or laying back on the ground, smoking cigarettes stolen from their dad.

'It's uncivilised, eating where you sleep,' Michael would persist.

'You eat in bed all the time!'

'I barely eat at all, which is why I'm ballerina skinny. And anyway, that was in the old world. With this den comes our New World Order. We're going to do things properly this time, you mark my words.'

'Not if we don't finish we're not.'

'You do it,' he'd say lazily. 'You're so strong and clever.'

'You're bone bloody idle,' Greg would huff. 'If you just lifted a finger then we'd be done in half the time.'

'I'll take care of the interiors. You're the brawn and I'm the brain.'

'The bane, more like.'

'Strong work, big man,' he would laugh, climbing high into the leaves above. 'Ten out of ten.'

Eventually, their den complete, the boys would sit quietly observing their handiwork.

'What do we do now?'

'We sit here and enjoy it,' Michael would say quietly, his eyes closing. 'This is our world now. It's just you and me.'

That night, and despite his father's protestations, they ate awkwardly in the newly renovated back yard, perched on kitchen chairs Greg had hauled outside before Teddy's return from work.

'It's all right, isn't it?' he said.

Greg had finished with just over an hour to spare before tea. He had showered and changed as quickly as he could, then hot-tailed it to the small supermarket on the high street, where he bought dinner for the evening, along with four bottles of beer to share.

On a small tray he carried out the oven pizza which he'd cut up into four, along with two plates, two beers poured into glasses and a bowl containing six rounds of slightly charred garlic bread.

'Where's all that going to go?' his dad asked as Greg made his way outside carrying the heaving tray.

'We'll just put it on the floor for now. You'll not need a knife and fork, it's only pizza. I'll get us a table once I've been paid. I've learned some card games at work. I can show you if you like.'

'I wouldn't worry about it,' he said. 'I doubt I'll be making a habit of this. Any chips?' Teddy had been at work all day, and felt a meal without chips was nothing short of an affront.

Greg sighed but did not let his father dampen his mood.

'No,' he said. 'I checked but they wanted a different gas mark to the pizza and the bread and I couldn't work it out. You can have my garlic bread if you like?' he offered as his father piled his plate high with precisely one half of the pizza and three quarters of the bread.

'I'll be starving come nine,' he objected, biting into the crust as a bee whizzed past his head.

Together they sat, balancing their meals on their laps in the dimming sun of the warm afternoon.

'I like it out here,' Greg said, which was true, though he had said it only to fill in the silence. 'Feels like we're on holiday.'

'That guttering wants sorting,' his dad said, pointing up at the black surround of the roof.

'Here,' Greg said, 'I got us these as well. It's a new beer. They're on offer at the moment. It's a special one.'

His father's face twisted at his first sip before he returned the glass to the ground, unimpressed.

'There's some lemonade in the cupboard if you don't like it?'

Teddy looked horrified.

'I've come this far in life without troubling a shandy,' he said staunchly. 'I do not intend to start now.'

'Fair enough,' said Greg. 'There's a can left in the fridge, do you want me to fetch that?'

His father shook his head, resolved to a meal without chips and a night without ale.

'So,' Greg said, 'there's this old boy at work. He's unreal. You'd like him. He's taken a shine to me. It was him that taught me the card games.'

He had no idea where exactly the story was heading but he felt like talking for the first time in a long time.

'What?' his dad snorted. 'Some old nonce, is he?'

Greg felt a fury build inside of him. On most nights he would have taken this as his cue, shrugging his father's cruelty and retreating wordlessly to bed. Tonight, however, he made the effort, though could not bring himself to let the slant pass entirely. Baxter had shown him affection. And for the first time in as long as Greg could remember, he had accepted it.

'No,' he said sharply, and then softened his tone. 'Why would you say that? Why . . . I mean, it's a weird thing to say, don't you think? He's my friend.'

'Just strange he wants a young lad as a friend, that's all,' Teddy said through a mouthful of bread. 'Is he married?'

Greg shook his head.

'Want to watch yourself with him then,' Teddy offered kindly towards his son. 'Sounds like a paedophile to me.'

Greg breathed deeply and forced himself to remain civil.

'Well, I'm nearly nineteen, so he'd be a pretty ineffectual one if I was his target,' he tried in a tone as light as he could muster.

'Pretty bloody desperate one more like it,' his father said, taking three deep glugs of the beer which had caused him such torment just two minutes prior.

Greg swallowed hard and continued.

'But he's really great for his age. He's like ninety or something

137

but you can't tell. And he's shit-hot on the piano. He can play anything you want, too, doesn't even need the music. He gave me a beginner's guide, in case I want to learn.'

'*You?*' his father asked incredulously. 'And anyway, there's no room here for a piano. Barely enough room for the book, truth be told. We've enough crap as it is.'

'Yeah, but just in case,' Greg said as his father checked his watch.

'It's blue bins tomorrow, you can chuck the book out before then and it can go with the rest of the rubbish,' he informed his son as Greg's heart sank.

'I'm trying here, Dad,' he said quietly.

Teddy's mind was already on other things.

'You're working tomorrow, aren't you?' he asked and Greg nodded. 'Good. I want you out and about. There's someone coming round to look at the house.'

'Why?' Greg asked, initially bemused before it hit him. '*No*,' he said. 'You're not selling it.'

Teddy finished his meal and returned his plate to the tray.

'It's too big for us,' Teddy said simply, finishing his beer. 'And it's not exactly dripping with good memories now is it?'

'But they're our memories,' Greg pleaded as his father stood up.

'You're so desperate to spread your wings? Well now's your time to fly.'

Greg felt anger simmer over from the part of his brain he could control.

'No!' he yelled, standing up and slamming his father's shoulders down, so that Teddy was forced to remain in his seat. 'Sit there and talk to me.'

His father was silent for a moment.

138

'Careful,' he said eventually, locking eyes with his son, though his strength had concerned him and he was cautious.

'Just once,' Greg said, holding back tears.

'What?' asked his father, uncomfortable with the flagrant display of emotion.

'Just once can't you just try and talk to me. Just be my dad. Be a human being.'

Greg's voice was quiet, as if he could diminish his emotions by regulating his own volume.

'This is no life. You don't enjoy anything. You work until you sleep and you sleep until you work. You eat to survive; you drink to disappear. Have you ever been happy?' he asked. 'Have you ever even been sad?' he went on, equally fascinated by his father's distance from life's necessary extremes. 'Your son walked into the woods and hung himself from a tree and you haven't once said a word about it. You go through the motions but it's not enough. You aren't ever kind to anyone. You're not even kind to me. I need you, Dad. I need somebody to look after me sometimes. But you can't even listen to me when I talk to you.'

'Not when you go on like this,' Teddy said, not so much in defence, rather out of genuine bemusement at his son's outburst.

'Not ever. It's horrible. I can't even tell you a stupid story about work without you ruining it or acting like it wasn't worth telling in the first place.'

'Life is hard,' his dad said.

'It's not a fucking endurance test!' Greg said on a growl of frustration as his father raised his eyes, silently intoning his displeasure at Greg's language. 'We're lucky, Dad, you and me. We're sat here. We've got a house. We've got jobs. The world we live in is safe . . . ish. We should be happy. We should at least try. You must be able to see that it's not right? The way we are? Don't you want to change? Don't you want to . . .' he tried, searching for the right word, '. . . live?'

He sat back into his seat, exhausted from his own outburst and certain that his father would at least comment upon the barrage he had witnessed.

'Well,' said Teddy, standing up once more, this time unobstructed by his eldest. 'If that's over and done with I'll be off out for a pint.'

Greg's entire body shook as he stood up alone in the garden. He forced the sadness that burned behind his eyes to cool, ignoring it as he had done all day with his nettle stings. He stacked the plates and glasses back on the tray, picking it up with unsteady hands. He heard the front door open and the latch secure, as his father made his way to the pub.

He turned and looked up at the house. The bathroom window was open, as was the window to Michael's room, though he could not remember opening it himself. He felt a tear roll down his cheek.

Turning back to the garden he smiled at his handiwork for the day, proud in spite of himself. Clearing his throat, he lifted the tray high up past his chest.

'Fuck it,' he said, before letting go and watching the tray slam full to the ground.

An explosion of glass and pottery skittered across his feet like rats fleeing their nest.

He turned and made his way back inside, locking the door behind him.

14

War was declared a week into Baxter's career.

Thomas was still in bed that morning as Baxter hurried to dress.

'Stay,' Thomas begged, pulling at Baxter's arm as he attempted to smarten his tie.

Baxter leant over and kissed him.

'I can't,' he replied. 'I'll be home by four. You may even be out of bed by then.' He brushed a stray strand of hair from Thomas's eyes.

'A kiss with a sting,' Thomas said, throwing himself back against the pillows and lighting a cigarette. 'Cruel, cruel fate.'

A bird started to sing in the eaves outside. Baxter felt a sudden rush – happiness and sadness hand in hand – as he stared down at the crumpled man in the crumpled bed, both irrevocably his.

'I expect an amusing anecdote upon your return,' Thomas yelled as Baxter made his way down the stairs to fetch his case.

'And I expect a cold gin and a warm welcome,' Baxter shot back, as Thomas rose from the bed and padded naked across the landing.

'Baxter!' he yelled, leaning over the bannister until his lover appeared, glancing nervously at his watch whilst he smoothed his jacket across his rigid arm.

'I'm late.'

'Good luck,' he said, and gave Baxter a wink.

Baxter felt his legs go weak.

'Thank you,' he said, momentarily glued to the spot.

'They're lucky to have you,' Thomas said as he made his way back to their shared quarters. 'I should know.'

The class seemed pleasant enough. The children were polite and proper. As a teacher, Baxter had a lot of ideas, but it would take a while to manifest them in the classroom. He believed music was as vital to children as reading or arithmetic. A love of sound and harmony at a young age instilled an awareness of themselves and the world around them. He'd seen it with Winnifred – through music came keenness of mind and heart. Now, she not only knew what she enjoyed, she also knew something of *why*.

His mind began to wander not long into the late-morning spelling lesson. While the children recited words by rote, in unison, his thoughts strayed to Thomas and the months which had passed in a blink of an eye.

The rhythm of the children's rhymes became hypnotic and it was only the sudden absence of sound that roused him from his daydream. The class sat in silence, staring expectantly up at him, their task complete.

'Very good,' he said. 'Once more for luck.'

The children began again, only to be stopped by the ringing of the lunchtime bell.

Baxter checked his watch and the clock above his desk. It

was not yet midday. Immediately alert to this unusual change of routine, the children murmured amongst themselves.

The classroom door opened and Mr Pearson stepped in with a nod to the children.

'Good morning, Mr Pearson,' the children said as one.

'An assembly has been called, Mr Baxter,' he informed the new teacher, who rose in his seat. 'In the dining hall, immediately.'

Thomas had become the go-to man about town for housewives whose husbands were weak on the DIY front. He could fix and build and clear and mend. He would refuse payment, though often the ladies would insist, keen not to be seen as taking a lend, and equally keen to retain the services of the handsome young man they'd glance hungrily at from behind twitching curtains.

'You've made quite the place for yourself,' Baxter said proudly one night in bed as the pair lay reading side by side. 'Mrs Hiscock could not speak highly enough of your skill with the hammer and nail.'

'If I make myself indispensable then I can't be asked to leave,' said Thomas, folding the page corner as he returned the book to his bed stand.

'Who'd ever ask such a thing?' Baxter asked, slipping down under the blankets. 'You've become quite vital.'

Winnifred, too, had taken to Thomas like a fish to water.

Always a robust child, she would clamber upon him and horseplay, pleased to have an equally vigorous partner in crime. No matter what the day held he was never too busy to play and she began to think of this new character as a gift for her and her only.

On warmer days and when their schedules allowed it, Baxter and Peggy would sit on the beach, burning their bare legs in the sun while they chatted away and ate sandwiches crunchy with sand. Thomas and Winnifred had no time for such boring pursuits as civilised conversation. So off they'd go, cartwheeling across the shore and throwing seaweed at one another before diving into water that stayed icy even in summer. The pair would swim out until Winnie became tired and was forced to wrap her arms around Thomas's neck as he hauled her back to shore.

'What will they say if we show up everywhere together?' Baxter fretted as Thomas fastened his tie one evening, stealing a kiss in the process before returning their glasses to the liquor cabinet.

'What do you mean?' Thomas asked, though of course he knew exactly.

'I mean we're not in some bacchanalian metropolis.'

'Could have fooled me,' Thomas said, standing behind Baxter and wrapping his hands around his waist, resting his chin on his lover's shoulder as he took in their reflection in the gilt mirror above the fireplace.

'Very good,' Baxter said, feeling Thomas's arms surrounding him, and easing into his embrace. 'But beyond these doors there are consequences for our actions.'

'Punishment for our wickedness.'

'It's a crime.'

'Yes,' Thomas said, in the most serious tone Baxter had ever heard him use. 'It is.'

'I just mean we must be careful. The world is not for our type.'

'Really?' Thomas asked, mocking and sceptical. 'Because it seems to me that our world starts at the front door and ends at the back yard. And it feels very much made for us and our type, whatever that may be.'

'But outside—'

'Does not matter,' he interrupted. 'The world ticks by with its own problems. Let's not worry. Let's just be thankful for what we have, here. Our space. A space that is safe. A space for two.'

Baxter nodded and turned to kiss Thomas's cheek.

'Very well,' he said. 'Let them think what they think.'

'Precisely,' Thomas said, unfurling from Baxter as he checked his own tie in the mirror. 'Besides, all I see is two confirmed bachelors out on the town,' he said, stretching out his arm and taking Baxter's hand in his, before letting go to check that his wallet was secure in his inside pocket.

'Look out, ladies,' Baxter said uncertainly, as Thomas laughed and pulled him in for one last kiss, before making their way out of their world and into the street to meet Peggy.

'Why has Mr Baxter yet to marry?' Winnifred asked, as her sister applied one last coat of red to her lips in the mirror. The girl lay on the bed, upside down, and watched with awe as her sister transformed into a creature too exquisite for the black and white world in which they lived.

Winnifred was to be watched that night by Mrs Hopkins, an elderly widow with a grim outlook and a quick temper who worked Tuesdays in the grocery store.

Peggy smiled at the sight of her face in the mirror, and at the girl's inquisitiveness. She tucked an auburn strand behind her ear and sprayed perfume across her collarbone.

'Some people,' she said, 'are not meant for a life on the track. Their path is different. Their fate is their own.'

'Like us?' tried Winnifred, sitting up.

'Quite,' said Peggy, making her way towards the bed where she had laid out her prettiest shawl. 'And some people want to see more of the world before they shut the door on it for ever,' she went on. 'Mr Baxter is one of them.'

Winnifred nodded in agreement. And whereas once her sister's logic would have made sense to her, recently she wasn't so sure.

'But he never leaves the house any more,' she objected and Peggy could not help but laugh.

'Some adventures require neither mast nor engine,' she said, tapping her nose as Winnie nodded wisely.

'He does have a lot of books . . . I shall see the world,' she said with certainty, 'and I shall never close my door on it, lest I miss one moment.'

'That's my girl,' Peggy said proudly, assuming it to be the end of the conversation.

Winnie was not done. 'For that matter, why have you yet to marry?' she asked, and Peggy shook her head.

'Because I make my own way and see no reason to change. Not all men like that in a woman.'

'Which do they dislike the most, your work or your stubbornness?' Winnie asked.

'Take your pick,' she said with a shrug, tilting her head from side to side, taking in her own beauty.

'I shall never wed,' Winnifred said indignantly, standing up on the mattress as if giving a speech. 'And I shall never grow old!' she declared, raising her arms to the roof to embellish the point.

'Oh, my girl,' Peggy said, scooping her up and holding her

tight to her chest. 'You will live to be one hundred years old, you mark my words. And what's more you'll enjoy every last moment of it,' she said, smelling the crown of her sister's head as if to take a small part of her with her.

'Promise?' Winnifred asked.

'Promise,' she said, and she meant it. 'There is a big, brilliant world out there, and in it a place for a girl just like you. Now,' she said, twirling so that her skirts fanned out. 'Will I do?'

'They don't deserve you,' Winnie said.

'Ain't that the truth, baby girl,' she said in the voice of the blues singer they both loved to listen to. 'Now hurry to bed before Mrs Hopkins arrives. The sooner you're asleep the less time you shall have to spend talking with her,' she instructed, hugging her sister and then gently slapping the back of her legs as she scuttled across the landing.

The housekeeper had been let go of once Baxter and Thomas's arrangement had become less formal. And so Thomas was left alone for eight long hours between Baxter's departure for work and his triumphant return that evening.

Nothing felt quite right without Baxter. The music he played seemed to echo back, as if the room itself was rejecting it. His thoughts went unspoken and unacknowledged until it felt as though he himself had disappeared. Without Baxter to watch him go about the myriad needless tasks he'd set for himself each day, none of it felt real.

He picked at the piano though no fresh melody came to him. He tidied the hallway and the living room, cluttered from an accumulation of two nights' worth of revels. With soap and water he wiped the floors and doorframes, and opened windows to let a breeze perk up the cushions and curtains that had become stale with smoke.

The radio was turned on and then off, once the news had been digested. He felt unable to listen to the constant repetition of the increasingly troubling developments. Instead, he would choose a record and play it as loud as possible while he prepared dinner for the evening and polished the glasses for Baxter's welcome-home drink.

He walked along Front Street, heading for the grocer's with a view to sharing tea and a natter with Peggy. Only to be disappointed to discover it was Mrs Hopkins' day behind the counter.

'If you aren't to buy then I bid you good day,' said Mrs Hopkins sternly, as Thomas failed spectacularly at initiating the old girl in conversation.

'I shall take the Brasso and some iron wool if you have it, Mrs Hopkins,' he said eventually, defeated in his efforts.

Back at the house he stripped to his vest and went at the dilapidated garden table and chairs, rendered dull by years of neglect and the stiff salt breeze, until they shone in the sun.

'There,' he said proudly, standing back and admiring the fruits of his labour, after almost two hours of condensed effort. 'Fit for a king.' He took a watering can to the beds, and picked a small colourful bouquet which he placed in a glass in the centre of the table.

He hurried to get the pie in the oven that night as the clock drew past Baxter's finishing time.

He poured two glasses of gin and set them on the table outside along with an apple for the teacher.

'Have you hired another housekeeper?' Baxter asked from

the hallway, as Thomas stood beside the garden chair, his face lighting up at the sound of his voice. 'The place is spotless.'

Thomas shook his head and pointed to himself.

'All me,' he said proudly, 'and look,' he said, gesturing towards the table.

'Resplendent.' Baxter nodded. Thomas pulled out a chair for him and insisted he sit. He removed his jacket and folded it across his lap as Thomas sat beside him and raised his glass.

'Welcome home, Mr Baxter,' he said, as they sipped their gin. 'And here, they say an apple for teacher does the trick. Who am I to argue?' He threw the russet up into the air for Baxter.

'Fool,' he said, taking a bite. 'My perfect fool.' Sitting back he felt the evening sun on his face, his feet heavy and swollen from his first full day of work.

'Dinner won't be long,' said Thomas. 'It's such a lovely evening I thought perhaps we could eat outside. Seems a shame to waste the table, after all my hard work.'

'Quite,' Baxter said, 'but what will the neighbours say?'

Thomas laughed.

'I'm not sure,' he said, standing up and collecting his glass, 'but whatever it is we won't be able to hear them if they're stuck inside now, will we?'

Baxter nodded at his reasoning though the prospect made him uneasy.

'Very good,' he said, 'and what's on the menu?' he asked as Thomas took his glass and apple core and made his way towards the house.

'Why don't you wash and ready yourself for supper, and I'll sort the rest. Then you can tell me all about your day.'

'I missed you,' Baxter said.

At first no reply came. Baxter, embarrassed, removed his spectacles and polished them on his sleeve to cut through the silence. Thomas had not meant to cause his beloved pain. He simply wanted time to take in the moment; to feel the happiness the way he felt the sun on his skin, and absorb the words like minerals, feeling nourished by their sincerity.

Finally it came. 'And I you, Mr Baxter,' he said, and vanished into the kitchen.

Thomas stood in the doorway holding a silver tray. On the tray were two plated slices of pie, along with a bowl of boiled potatoes and two napkins.

'What a sight,' said Baxter.

'Myself? Or the food?' Thomas asked.

'Pick one,' Baxter said, taking a sip of wine.

'So then, my boy. What news?' asked Thomas, and Baxter sighed before recanting his day from beginning to end.

He told Thomas of the children and his fellow teachers, affecting voices and facial expressions to emphasise the humour in what had been a strange, humourless day.

'And then the bell tolled,' Baxter said as they placed their cutlery onto empty plates. 'We were taken to the hall for an assembly. The news . . .'

'I know,' Thomas said, shaking his head. Keen to stave off what was fast approaching for at least another evening. 'I know,' he said again, stretching his hand and brushing it twice against Baxter's thigh.

'What will become of us if we go to war?' Baxter asked.

Thomas shook his head as the sun dipped across the estuary, casting an orange beam which wrapped the horizon like a bow.

'Let morning bring news,' he said quietly, relaxing further into his chair. 'For now, tonight, let's enjoy it while we can.'

Baxter closed his eyes, his mind cleared by the chirping of the gulls in the distance. 'I wish I could live this moment for ever. This moment, right now, with you, for ever.'

'Yes,' Thomas said quietly, his voice deep with tiredness. 'But if the moment must pass – and it must – then at least we'll hold the memory. No matter what happens, your happiness cannot be taken from you, Mr Baxter. And in you I've known the greatest happiness of all. I feel it only right you must know.'

Beneath the table Baxter reached out and took Thomas's hand in his.

15

Ramila's head grew heavy and dropped as she sat at reception.

Her start time was six, and at twenty past she had arrived with eyes like pinholes to relieve the desperate agency staff member who preceded her that morning.

'Don't even start, Jimmy,' Ramila had said as Jimmy, a polite older gentleman whose skill set didn't extend far beyond answering telephones and shrugging, collected his things. 'I know, I know . . .' she said, defending herself pre-emptively against the scolding that would never come. 'I'm late, fine, whatever. But in my defence, I've adapted my body clock to work to the best of my abilities during my usual hours, so it's actually really selfless of me to be here at all and, quite frankly, careless of management to roster me on an early.'

'There's coffee already made,' Jimmy offered, collecting his carrier bag of half-eaten sandwiches and half-read paperbacks.

She scanned the darkened corridors either side of the desk. Most of the lights, save the constant burners, had yet to burst into being and the gloomy solitude made her uneasy.

'Stay and talk to me,' she begged

'I've an appointment,' he said uncertainly, eyeing the ground.

'Nobody has an appointment at this hour, James,' she said with a snarl, leaning forwards on her elbows as poor Jimmy seemed to recoil on the spot. 'That cuts, my friend. That cuts deep. Rejected and it's not even –' she checked her watch – '*seven.*'

She had tried her hardest to occupy herself but still the minutes dragged.

She had live-tweeted her ordeal, implementing her own hashtag, only to be offended by the startling lack of activity over her episodic suffering. She had left the confines of the desk to carry out a rise-and-shine exercise class on one of the breakfast TV shows, but gave up halfway though, breathless and sweating, and chain-smoked three cigarettes off the belt in order to realign her nerves, one foot jamming the front door open for form's sake.

Greg's backpack hung heavy as he made his way out of the house and down the street.

The milkman was still delivering, and the light was clear and undisturbed as he blinked sleep from his eyes. Greg had not showered that morning, keen not to wake his dad. Instead he passed a flannel across his body over the sink, and doubled his usual blast of deodorant before eating a cold slice of bread standing up in the kitchen, with one thought and one thought only passing through his mind ad infinitum:

What the fuck am I doing . . .?

He made it to the end of his street, paused, took hold of his senses and retraced his steps, arriving back at his front door with a poised key. From the landing on the other side of the door he heard a creak. He looked up at his father's bedroom – the light was switched on and the top window was open.

Greg contemplated his key, his stomach knotted, before turning his back on home for a second time. He made it all the way to Melrose Gardens this time. No pausing. No backtracking.

Ramila saw Greg approach on the security cameras which pointed both left and right of the main entrance. She watched him walk with his head bowed until he reached the door.

'Morning,' he said, only slightly breathless from his walk. 'You all right?'

Ramila raised her head pitifully from the desk.

'Gregory,' she croaked. 'My prince. My saviour. I called and you came . . .'

'Suzanne got you to do an early then?' he said as Ramila stretched limply across the desk and took Greg's arm in hers.

'I don't know how long I've been here. What time is it? What day? What year? I'm so weak and bored. Please help me.'

'It's only half seven,' Greg said, checking the morning television clock. 'I thought you only started at six?'

Ramila sat up and took a sip of her coffee.

'I thought I was a goner,' she said, shaking her head. 'But now you're here, and I'm saved. Praise be to the Lord on high.'

'I can't stop,' he said.

'You're at work,' Ramila said, suddenly not so limp. 'You've got to stay. It's your contractual obligation. That you get to save my life in the process is a bonus.'

Greg shuffled on the spot for a moment as Ramila stared him down.

'Talk to me,' she said with a whine as the timers kicked in and the corridors burst into sickly light.

'*See*,' she said. 'The angels are keen to take me, Greg. My future is in your hands.'

Greg checked the time again nervously. 'I can do you a coffee if you like but that's it.'

'I don't need a *coffee*,' she said, sitting back and draining her cup. 'What I need is an act of kindness from a man I love – *that's you, Greg* – to bring me back to life.'

'It'll wake you up.'

'I've already had five,' Ramila said.

'Five?' Greg checked and she nodded proudly. 'Anyway, that's all I can offer you today. I've got an arrangement.'

'What's with the backpack?' she asked, moving from self-indulgence to curiosity.

Greg blushed and shrugged. He was no good when put on the spot. He could not spin pithy yarns to get himself out of trouble. His brother had been the pro in that department.

'Just easier to carry stuff around with,' he said and made his way towards the corridor. Ramila caught his arm and gripped with the determination of a boa constrictor, forcing him to the spot.

'Yes,' she pushed, 'the principle of the backpack is one I'm familiar with. What troubles me,' she went on, 'is where it fits in with your activities for today?'

Greg was silent. Ramila did not release her grip.

'I really need to go, Ramila,' he said nervously. 'Please,' he tried.

'Something is up,' she said, picking up her notepad and rustling the paper enthusiastically. 'I can feel it. I shall let you pass, Gregory, but I'm not one bit happy about being excluded. Not one goddamn bit, you hear me?'

'Cheers, Ramila,' he said, bolting towards the staircase, aware that a delay in the lift arriving could herald another swift change in her attitude.

'Gregory,' Baxter answered the door, indignant at having been left waiting until the last minute for an answer. 'You never got back to me. I was sound asleep.'

Greg stepped into his room.

'Were you fuck, you're already dressed,' he said, placing his bag beside Baxter's on the bed before catching his own tone. '*Sorry*,' he added. 'It's just early, that's all.'

'Yes well, you got lucky.'

'Is that a thank you?' Greg asked.

Baxter harrumphed as he slid his wallet and passport into his inside pocket.

'If you like,' he said, dragging his comb across his head before slipping it carefully next to his wallet. 'Hand me that aftershave on the nightstand, will you.'

Gregory picked through the bottles of scents and potions clustered on the small table.

'What made you decide to come?' Baxter asked, spritzing his lapels before checking through the front pocket of his carry-on bag to make sure there were no last-minute essentials he had forgotten.

'Dunno really,' said Greg, stealing a spray of the cologne for himself. 'I just thought about what you said.'

'I am very wise,' Baxter said as Greg sat down.

'Give it a rest, Baxter, it's too early for this. Do you need anything doing before we go?' he asked as Baxter zipped his bag and checked himself once more in the mirror.

'I thought we'd take breakfast here,' he offered. 'I'm paying for the privilege, may as well make the most of it.'

Greg shook his head.

'No can do,' he said staunchly. 'Suzanne starts at half eight. If I see her, even if I think she might catch us, I'm out. I know it. So if we're doing this, whatever it is this is, we need to go and we need to go now.'

'You like her, don't you?'

'She's kind, and she listens. I feel bad doing this. Like, properly bad. Like I still don't think it's a good idea.'

'Very well,' Baxter said. 'I shall call a taxi and we will eat breakfast at the station. My treat.'

'This whole thing is your treat,' Greg said. 'I've only got about a tenner.'

'Wonderful,' said Baxter, straightening his tie. 'On your feet then. My bag isn't too heavy so you should have no difficulty managing it along with yours.'

The pair skipped past reception as the taxi honked its horn outside.

'Where do you think you're going?' Ramila asked as Greg made his way towards the waiting car and threw himself in the back seat.

'Best you don't know,' Baxter said. 'I'd tell you, but I'd have to kill you.'

'Are you doing a runner?' she asked. '*Without me?*'

'A temporary respite, my dear. If I could take you with me I would, but alas.'

Ramila shook her head. 'Fine. I wouldn't even want to come anyway. It sounds *shit* whatever it is.'

'Rest assured you'll be first in line for my next escapade,' Baxter said, halfway out of the door. 'But be a dear and stave off any news of our departure for as long as you can.'

'I take it you mean Suzanne.'

'You always were a smart one,' said Baxter, as the driver leant over and opened the front passenger door. 'It's why I like you so much.'

Ramila watched the car accelerate and then disappear from view.

'Little bastards,' she said. 'Sneaky little bastards,' she said again, and returned to the text she had been sending.

Baxter paid the taxi driver with a note and did not wait for his change.

'Thank you, sir,' he said, stepping out of the car with his walking stick as Greg balanced the bags either side of him.

The driver's attempts at chatter had been largely met with one-word answers and indifferent nods from Greg, who struggled with small talk at the best of times, but found it near excruciating on the first leg of a mystery tour at an hour he had not been familiar with for some time.

Fortunately for all involved, Baxter was nothing if not loquacious, albeit on his terms, and had managed to initiate a discussion which he felt comfortable enough to preside over for the three miles it took to get to Central Station.

'Fat lot of good you were back there,' he said to Greg as they made their way through the glass doors and the sandstone arches that formed the altar of the station. 'Aah,' said Baxter, looking up at the architecture as though it were a work of art. 'Beautiful, isn't it?'

'It's all right I suppose,' Greg said, hauling the bags across the pavement. 'Big.'

'We're all in such a hurry, head down, charging on, day in day out. It would be quite easy to miss a sight as mighty as this. One must always remember to look up, Gregory,' said Baxter, breathing deeply as though absorbing the wisdom of his own words before marching onwards towards the main stretch of the station. 'Come. We haven't got all day,' he said, as the boy hoisted the bags back onto his shoulder and scuttled after the old man.

'You going to tell me what this is all about then?' Greg asked, as he and Baxter sat in a station café eating breakfast. Baxter had, after grimacing at the offerings, settled on a chocolate croissant and a black coffee. Greg made his way through a bacon sandwich with extra black pudding and a pot of tea for two.

'Of course,' Baxter said. 'Of course. But all in good time. I can't concentrate with this bloody racket, let alone articulate my life's story.' He glanced angrily at the overhead tannoy.

'Give it a go,' Greg said. 'Even just a bit of it.'

'I will say that my mission is one of love.'

'You're off to see some old flame?'

Baxter nodded and smiled.

'Well, in part, yes. I'm to pay respects which should have been paid decades ago,' he said.

The announcer carried on repeating their urgent mantra despite a wiring issue that made even the most emphasised words sound distorted and hazy.

'Have you ever felt drawn to a place you've never been to before?'

Greg thought for a moment and nodded. The chill of the

160

station echoed the cold dread he felt each time he found himself back in the woods.

'Yes,' Greg said certainly. He was not one for raking over the past in the company of others. In his solitary hours his memories played on repeat like a title screen he was too exhausted to switch off. But the thought of sharing any of it with another was unthinkable. And yet Baxter was different. He hadn't felt so comfortable with another human being since his brother had passed away. In Baxter, Gregory felt like somebody cared. So he took a risk.

'Where Michael died. In the woods. Sometimes it's like my body takes me there and I don't know why, like a magnet or something. But I just can't *not* go, at least not at the moment. He was always demanding as fuck, our Michael. Hasn't even stopped now that he's dead. The little twat.'

Baxter closed his eyes and forced himself to keep his composure at the boy's honesty. For some time he had suspected that Greg's pain had, in a roundabout way, the same quality as his. Each man had known their first loves, their true loves, extinguished without explanation. A loss so sudden and so cruel is a loss one must survive each day, every day. It is a brave soul who finds the strength to do so.

Baxter looked at Greg, over cooling coffee and limp pastries. There was a resilience in him that Baxter recognised. It was this strength which would carry him through, even when he felt like giving up.

'Precisely,' Baxter said. 'And whilst one cannot explain the lure of such whims, we cannot deny the benefit of adhering to them at times, either. Wouldn't you agree?'

'I suppose.'

161

'Then you understand. Life has a way of turning you into someone that you sometimes don't even recognise as yourself; so different from the character you assumed you'd grow into. I suppose I am fortunate, in a way. I can pinpoint on a map the spot on which my course was forever altered. I should like to visit it. To see where I started before I ultimately end, I suppose.'

'That's bleak.'

'Such is life,' said Baxter, sighing with relief as the overhead tannoy fell silent. 'And if those I held dear aren't remembered now, by me, there's a chance they shall disappear when I do. And we can't be having that now, can we?'

'I wish I'd had you around when our Michael killed himself,' Greg said bluntly, certain of the thought he felt could not be left unsaid. 'You know more than anyone who's ever tried to speak to me about it.'

Baxter smiled.

'It comes with age, Gregory. Believe me when I say that my own grief was handled nowhere near as well as yours was. You've done just fine without me and you shall continue to do so long after I'm gone. You're a good person. It's not your fault, you can't help it, no matter how bloody hard you try. But it's a rare quality, your goodness, and one that will see you through even the most trying of times.'

'I hope so,' Greg said, finishing his sandwich and draining his last cup of tea.

Baxter placed his wallet back in his inner pocket and took hold of his walking stick. The station was bustling now and the voice on the overhead speakers, though no less intrusive, had at least become recognisably human. Their train was running on

162

time, as fortune would have it, and would be departing in just over twenty minutes.

'It's all worthwhile,' Baxter said, rising to his feet. 'There's a big world out there, Gregory, and believe it or not it's not all awful. In fact, and I don't say this nearly enough, it's actually rather lovely.'

'Yeah? Well. Fingers crossed, eh?' Greg said, collecting the bags and, as an afterthought, pocketing the spare sugar sachets in case of emergencies in the strange new land he was heading towards.

'No luck required,' Baxter said, 'and I know everything so you shall take my word for it. Now hurry along with those bags. Behave yourself and I shall treat you to a periodical for the journey.'

16

The carriages were all but full by the time the train reached Newcastle.

'Lord have mercy,' Baxter said, as they made their way unsteadily towards their seats.

The sound of a baby crying created the relentless bassline to the cacophony of the train. Towards the back, where Greg struggled to wedge their bags into the suitcase crate, a stag do chanted songs and toasted with breakfast beers. Behind them an electronic door had come loose of its programming and clapped an unsteady rhythm out of sync with the train's juddering ascension.

'This is unacceptable,' Baxter said, gripping the headrest of an unoccupied seat for support as he dramatically pressed a handkerchief to his nose.

'Give over,' said Greg. 'Look. We've booked seats. We've a table to ourselves. Just sit down and stop making a fuss. It's fine.'

In front of them a family – mum, dad, two young boys – sat

around a table strewn with sandwiches, juice boxes and the scrawled-on corpses of newspapers. A wrestling match was developing between the children. Their mother presided half-heartedly while their father dozed oblivious, with one hand resting on the head of a whippet whose racing days had long since passed.

'It absolutely is not fine,' said Baxter. 'These people defy natural selection!'

Greg kicked his shin beneath the table as sincerely as he could without breaking one of his dusty old bones.

'*Enough*,' he whispered sharply, glancing up and down the carriage in embarrassment. 'You're going to get us done in. Or kicked off. Either way you're helping no one.'

'I know,' said Baxter, quieter this time. 'But it's just all so sad. In my day, there was an elegance to train travel. That's why I chose it. We could easily have flown but I thought rail would add to the sense of occasion.'

Greg smiled and shook his head. 'You've never quite been part of this world, have you, Mr Baxter?'

'Certainly not this one, no,' he said sadly, picking at a mound of sugar ingrained on the Formica table.

'If you think this is bad I'd love to see you on a budget airline,' said Greg.

'No doubt it would cause my ultimate demise,' Baxter conceded. 'But still . . . who's going to write a romance set on a train these days, when this is what we're presented with.'

The voice overhead began listing the myriad stops separating them from London King's Cross, as Greg removed his hoodie and placed it on the window seat, keen to deter a third party from encroaching.

'Yeah, well, we're not here to fall in love, are we? We're here to get somewhere. So sit down and be nice.'

Suzanne was finishing up her morning rounds of the first floor. She went door to door with her dispensing trolley as usual, calling on every resident out of kindness and handing out medication to those as needed it. Baxter's room was her last stop.

She tapped gently.

'Hello, flower, it's just me,' she said quietly at the keyhole. 'Angel of the morning here to make your dreams come true. Can I come in?' she tried again, and then called his name with a degree of worry in her voice. Even at his most objectionable Baxter was not one to let social graces slip.

'You all right, flower?' she yelled this time. 'Do you need some help?'

When there was no answer forthcoming she quickly reached to her pocket and struggled with her keys.

Inside, the room was still and the window was shut. His bed had been made and his belongings remained exactly in place. His day-to-day medicine separator had gone from the dressing table. A Boots bag had been relieved of its contents and was scrunched in the waste bin, along with several balled drafts of a letter.

The only incongruity she could see – other than the fact that Baxter was not there – was a small white envelope resting on the pillow. Further inspection revealed that it was her name written on the front.

'This had better be a suicide note,' she mumbled, as she prised open the seal.

Dear Suzanne

Our talk was most beneficial and on balance I feel better for it. However, I'm afraid I must ignore your concerned warning and carry on as planned.

I shan't be gone long, and look forward to the sight of your winning smile upon my return. Though I am aware that technically I am in your care, and that my leave will incur certain administrative efforts on your part, please consider this letter proof that I am sound of body and mind and safe in my endeavours.

All concerns or repercussions can be forwarded to myself, and shall be dealt with promptly upon my return.

All the very best

Mr Baxter

Suzanne read the letter, re-read it and read it once more before folding it tightly and slipping it into the breast pocket of her overalls.

She took in the room and the warming day outside. She breathed in and closed her eyes momentarily, enjoying the distant sound of birdsong. Then, turning on her heel and shutting the door behind her, she kicked the stoppers from her trolley and made her way back towards the lift.

'Shit,' she said.

'I don't know a thing!' Ramila said in a panic when she saw Suzanne storming towards her.

'I thought as much,' Suzanne said, making her way behind the desk, checking that they were alone and glaring at Ramila with steely intent. '*Speak.*'

'Look, I'm sworn to secrecy, Suzanne.'

'*Ramila*,' Suzanne warned her as the girl groaned and held her head in her hands.

'Ramila, my love,' she tried again through a rictus grin. 'One of my residents has gone, and I've a feeling you know which one. Now, I adore this little routine you've got going on, but if you don't start telling me exactly what I need to hear then I'm going to put you through that fucking wall. Do you understand?'

Ramila nodded. 'They got a taxi this morning. About an hour before you got in,' she said, as Suzanne's worst fears were confirmed, compounded and augmented in one fell swoop.

'*They?*' she asked.

'Greg,' Ramila said. 'He went with him.'

'Fantastic. Just bloody fantastic.'

'Oh, Suzanne, you're not going to fire him, are you?' Ramila begged as Suzanne stood up and collected some essentials from the desk. 'He's lovely, our Greg. And he's got a crush on me which really helps with my low self-esteem. Plus . . .'

Suzanne raised her hand to demand silence. 'Rest assured that little shit will be begging for the sweet release of termination once I'm done with him.'

'Go easy.'

'And where was it heading?' she asked, ignoring Ramila's pleas for mercy. '. . . the taxi?' she added.

Ramila looked dumbstruck.

'Beyond what I've told you I'm legitimately clueless,' she said and Suzanne nodded once.

'That I believe,' she said. 'Now I'm going into the back and I shan't be out for some time. So you're glued to this desk and you're not to say a word about any of this to anybody until I tell you otherwise. Do you understand?'

Suzanne sat down in her office and turned on her desktop computer, opening as many Google tabs as she could focus on at once.

She was furious at the situation but not at all surprised by it. Baxter was his own man, for good or ill. It wasn't the paperwork or the flack she'd have to face that caused her such dismay. In truth what smarted was the fact that he had known her feelings and gone ahead regardless. Still, she thought, at least he had left a note, and a handwritten one at that. It showed a degree of respect.

On one hand the entire thing was an unnecessary headache to her; but on the other she knew Baxter's journey mattered to him and mattered greatly. And deep down, she rather wished him well.

With a sigh, Suzanne placed a one hundred and twenty-minute alert on the stopwatch setting of her mobile.

'You've got two hours' head start, you pair of sods,' she mumbled, before popping the phone discreetly back inside of her bra. 'I'll give you that by the grace of my kind nature. After that you're on your bloody own.'

Baxter tried to focus on his book while Greg stared out of the window contemplating one staggeringly obvious thought: the world was big and there was so much of it he hadn't seen, even right on his doorstep.

Shortly after York the trolley service made its way around for a second time having restocked its supplies.

'Would you like another coffee?' the man in uniform asked, clearing Baxter's empty paper cup and Greg's crumpled can from the table.

Baxter looked up and shook his head.

'My boy,' he offered, solemnly. 'Rations and Zeppelins made my generation tough, but even I could not suffer that ordeal twice over.'

'We're all right, thanks,' Greg said, glaring at Baxter.

'Still managed to finish it I see,' said the bored server as he unclipped the stoppers from his wheels.

'And it is testament to my survival instincts that I did.'

'They are funny when they get to that age,' the man said to Greg with a smile as he made his way past.

'Maybe funny but not necessarily deaf, now bugger off!'

The mother from the adjoining table leant over and clicked her fingers at Baxter.

Greg sunk lower into his seat.

''Scuse me mate,' she said in a lilting, cockney accent, 'can you watch the language in front of the kids? It's not on, that,' she said, nudging her sleeping husband.

'Sorry,' Greg said, hoping to nip it in the bud.

'I beg your pardon,' Baxter said. 'Do you mean to tell me for one moment that you find *our* behaviour unacceptable?'

Greg felt his insides knot.

'I don't want the kids picking up bad habits,' she said, nodding at the pair, who had taken to beating one another with rolled-up magazines. 'Got to be careful.'

'Yes,' Baxter conceded, 'though perhaps if they expanded their vocabulary they would not need to resort to such behaviour to settle disputes.'

'Who the hell do you think you are?' she asked, as Baxter shrugged away her outrage and looked out of the window.

'Look, we'll keep it down, all right,' Greg said. 'OK? I've said sorry.'

'Yeah, but he bloody didn't though,' she said, and Baxter hooted at her expletive.

'Careful,' he whispered. 'Don't want them picking up any bad habits.'

'Aye, you want to watch they're not getting any funny ideas,' Greg added.

'You want to be ashamed of yourselves. I won't be told how to raise my family by some old poof and his fat fancy boy,' said the woman.

Baxter chuckled to himself as she plugged in a pair of earphones and simmered down to mutual, wordless seething.

'Well,' he said, 'I must take advantage of the facilities. Keep an eye on our belongings, Gregory.'

Baxter scanned both exits of the carriage before heading towards the front of the train.

'The other way's closer, Baxter,' Greg said, as the old man shuffled off, ignoring him.

Baxter made his way through four carriages and past six entirely vacant toilets before reaching a vestibule where he leant to one side of the glass door and began to pant. Bent over, he pressed his hand to his head, rubbing his temples with his thumb and forefinger whilst his breathing deepened and his stance lowered. Gripping tightly to his walking stick he removed his hand from his head and pressed it to his chest, inching it towards the left and massaging the spot above his heart.

At the other side of the carriage two of the on-board team members stood chatting.

'Uh-oh,' said Melanie, glancing over Paul's head through first class, and catching a glimpse of the struggling old man. 'Looks like we've got trouble. Are you all right, love?' she asked, taking Baxter gently by the elbow as he huffed and puffed, his hand shaking across his chest.

'I . . . I,' he tried, 'I don't know where I am. My stick,' he said, shaking the apparatus. 'I must sit.'

'Sure, sure,' said Melanie, leading him into first class and placing him at an empty table.

Baxter nodded his appreciation and sank back into the comfort of his new seat, carefully breathing in short, faltering breaths.

'I'm so sorry for the inconvenience,' he said. 'I should try to head back but I can't remember . . .'

'Nonsense,' said the woman. 'We've plenty of space here. Do you have any medicine with you? Anything you should be taking?' she asked as Baxter shook his head.

'At my age it's mostly a wing and a prayer,' he said and Melanie laughed sweetly.

'You look like you're doing all right to me. Just need to get your sea legs yet, that's all. You sit here and I'll have someone go and fetch your bags.'

'If it's not too much trouble,' Baxter said meekly, handing her his ticket so that she could observe his initial seat number. 'My grandson, Gregory, he has my belongings. I feel such an old fool . . .'

'I'll have him along here in no time. If you need anything at all while you wait you just give my friend Paul here a shout.'

'Thank you, my dear,' Baxter said, slipping a five-pound note into Melanie's hand.

'I can't take that,' she said. 'I'm only doing my job.'

'Nonsense,' Baxter said. 'You've gone above and beyond. You're a testament to your vocation.'

'Bless you,' she said, accepting the gift and standing up. 'Nobody ever says thank you any more. You just make sure you don't go anywhere until I'm back.'

Melanie squeezed Baxter's shoulder as she made her way towards standard class.

'I'll be here,' he said timidly. '*God willing*,' he added, for good measure.

When Melanie was out of sight he sat back up in his chair and regained his posture.

'Oh, Paul,' he yelled. 'A word, if you'd be so kind . . .'

By the time Greg arrived in first class, Baxter had arranged a complimentary feast for them both.

'All right, *granddad*,' Greg said, placing their bags in the roomier overhead compartments and sitting down. 'You feeling better?'

There was a cup of coffee for Baxter and a can of pop for Greg. Two types of biscuit were nestled alongside plastic trays of triangle sandwiches and packets of artisanal crisps. Two scones had been sliced, buttered and spread thick with clotted cream and jam.

'Barely,' Baxter said. 'But I put a brave face on it.'

'It's all you can do,' Greg said, watching Baxter nibble the edge of a scone.

'He had a little bit of a scare,' said Melanie, as Greg took a sip of his drink.

'Blood sugar no doubt,' Baxter said. 'It's my diabetes.' He looked up at Melanie forlornly. '*The silent killer.*'

'If only,' Greg said, slumping back into his seat as he glowered at Baxter.

They made their way through Yorkshire's green expanse in relative silence.

'Oh, come on,' Baxter said after a while. 'I did all right, didn't I? Just admit it,' he said, nodding towards the spread as Greg smirked and took a sandwich.

'I thought something had happened to you.'

Baxter nodded.

'I apologise,' he said, 'though it was a necessary evil.'

'If you wanted an upgrade you should have just proposed to me. Would have been a lot easier.'

'Not sure you'd have said yes,' Baxter said. 'And besides, I forgot the ring.'

'So are you then?' said Greg after a while. 'You know what that awful missus said? *Some old poof?*'

Baxter laughed at his imitation of her estuary accent.

'So rude to comment upon an individual's age. But yes, that would be one epithet, I daresay. Though not one I care for entirely.'

'Cool,' Greg said.

'Isn't it just?' Baxter said.

'So is it a bloke we're off to visit then?' Greg asked, peeling open a packet of vegetable crisps and recoiling in horror at the shards of salted swede.

Baxter thought for a moment and nodded.

'A man,' he said. 'The best there was.'

'*Was?*'

'Was,' Baxter said sadly, and Greg nodded.

'So he didn't make it then?'

'The best never do,' Baxter said, as the train announced its imminent arrival in Doncaster. 'It's us also-rans who are left to pick up the pieces. Do the best we can with the lessons they taught us.'

'True that,' Greg said.

They were quiet for a moment and Baxter picked at the crisps discarded by Greg.

'Our Michael was too,' Greg said eventually. 'A poof. I mean homosexual. I mean ... gay?'

He turned and stared intently out of the window.

'I'd have liked to have met him,' Baxter said sincerely. 'Winnie was very taken by young Michael. She's not easily won over, let me tell you, so I feel it only right you know how much of a mark he made there, and how much she cared. I know she wishes it had been enough ...'

Greg shrugged and blinked back tears.

'She cared more than she had to,' he added. 'It was everyone else ...' he said, and stopped himself.

'The world,' Baxter said slowly, 'is a lot kinder now than when I was his age – but not yet kind enough, I'm afraid. What happened to your brother was wrong, Gregory. I can understand how hard it is for you to comprehend any of it. You're one of the good ones, which is a blessing, but it makes the badness even more of a mystery.'

Greg sniffed and shook his head.

'I'm not good,' he said, and when Baxter went to interrupt Greg carried on regardless. 'I've done bad things. Do you know that? I put three people in hospital. Did Ms Milliner tell you that? Nearly killed one of them, too. Would have if his brother hadn't been there. Would have killed him on the spot,' he said, wiping away a tear. 'A good person couldn't do that.'

'Yes,' Baxter said, 'he could. That's the human part, I'm afraid, the mess and violence and instances of ... *screwing up*, so to speak. It's something we're none of us immune to. Your anger was justified, but it manifested itself the wrong way. A bad person would not have felt remorse afterwards.'

'Yeah, well, I wasn't good enough to keep him alive.'

'Nonsense,' Baxter whispered firmly. 'I know your brother had a hard life, Winnifred told me as much. I know he knew hardship and distress. But that wasn't all. He also knew happiness, one way or another, and from what I hear, that happiness was largely down to you, Gregory.'

Another tear rolled down Greg's face as Baxter began tidying the remnants of their lunch into a smaller pile on the table.

'You think so?' he said. 'Because it doesn't always feel that way.'

'You didn't fail. And nor did he.'

'Cheers, Baxter,' Greg said, sitting up in his seat.

'I just told you what you already knew,' he said, giving Greg a wink as he drew his cup close to his lips, sipped, then spluttered, scowled and slammed the cup straight back down.

'What's the matter now?' Greg asked

'It's the same fucking coffee!' he said, and groaned in his seat like a chastised infant.

Suzanne flinched for a moment before remembering her alarm.

Retrieving the phone from its snug in her bra she turned off the caustic buzz and breathed in deeply.

'Right you are then,' she said quietly to herself, closing her files. 'Get a move on, you old fox. I'm releasing the hounds.'

She tidied the desk around her and swilled her mouth with cold remnants of tea before picking up the landline and dialling the non-emergency police number. Mr Patel would be next on her list, the call she was keenest to avoid, but with all paperwork filed and all relevant authorities informed, he would be limited in his outrage as to her part in the fiasco.

They answered on the third ring, and Suzanne drew a heavy breath before continuing.

'Hello, love,' she said, overly brightly. 'My name's Suzanne. I'd like to report a missing person. Nothing too serious. I'm a manager at Melrose Gardens Care Home.'

'And how long have they been missing for?'

Suzanne did the maths in her head.

'Seven hours,' she answered, 'give or take.'

The operator sighed and the sound of the keyboard slowed to a stop.

'What makes you think they're missing, Susan?' she asked drolly. 'Is it possible they're just out for the day?'

Suzanne breathed deeply.

'Oh no,' she said, confident yet breezy. 'You just trust me on this one. He's gone all right.'

On the other end of the line the sound of typing resumed.

17

One by one, the boys of Baxter's home town were called up over the following years.

As an educator, Baxter's role was reserved. He would not be uprooted and yet the streets he had walked his whole life had begun to feel so alien. Each stray sound became a cause for alarm. Every clank and boom, no matter how familiar, was a potential apocalypse in which luck was your only hope.

Thomas, being of no fixed occupation, was not so fortunate. Although he was a pacifist, he knew that should his call-up come he would rise to meet his duty, despite Baxter's pleas.

The subject arose time and again between the pair, for it weighed heavy.

'Say you go off to the front. What then?' Baxter asked one sleepless night, as a siren blared in the distance. Thomas, lying beside him, slid his hand across Baxter's stomach.

'It's freedom we're fighting for. You may not believe in war but surely you believe in that?'

'I'm not sure what I believe nowadays. This is all I know any more,' he said, moving closer so that Thomas's chin rested on his shoulder. 'The thought of it disappearing . . . I just can't place this in the context of some global bloodbath. I can't bring myself to care about the world beyond this bed.'

Thomas kissed his jaw.

'We could abscond. Move abroad,' Baxter said, in all seriousness. 'I have enough money, should it come to it.'

'The war would find us,' Thomas said, and even in the dark Baxter could tell that his eyes were closed.

'We're good at hiding,' said Baxter, and Thomas let out a single, breathy laugh.

'This is a different kettle of fish, my love.'

'I'll find a way to stop it,' Baxter said.

'The war?' asked Thomas. 'You're crazy. Insane. A complete and utter madman.'

'You make me so,' Baxter said, turning onto his side, though making sure Thomas did not retrieve his arm from its spot across his waist.

'And what a beautiful malady to behold,' Thomas said, gently kissing the top of Baxter's neck, beneath the bristle of his hairline. 'Now sleep.'

Peggy found that war drove her to a level of exhaustion she had never imagined possible.

The store was inundated with custom. She was sure to reclaim her outgoings to the penny, but it was disheartening to carry out so many transactions in ink and stamps – marking the ration books and turning away those who tried to cheat the stringent rules. She missed most the rewarding clink of coins in the till.

Alongside her role as the town's sole dispenser of rations, she somehow became the go-to girl for local ladies in need of an ear. Mothers pining for their boys and wives lost without their husbands would pour their hearts out to her across the counter when it came their turn in the queue.

This marked a turning point for Peggy. The same ladies who now sought out her company had not always been so friendly. They had arched their eyebrows the moment her figure had sprouted, and raised them further still when she chose to remain unwed and staunchly independent following her parents' death.

Now, her reputation was re-evaluated. Her stoicism shone through and her efforts went above and beyond the call of duty. She would open early and close late, and make deliveries to those who found the short journey too much to bear. Against every rule in the book and often at her own expense, extra rations would be held back and gifted to those who had received telegrams in lieu of reunions.

Baxter and Thomas also found a new role in the local community when they began to grow plants not just for pleasure, but for survival.

Former flowerbeds were dug up and in their place grew runner beans and carrots, radishes and persistent rhubarb. In summer they yielded strawberries which they preserved and jarred. And on cruel winter mornings they plucked potatoes from the frozen earth with their bare hands, filling the basket before rushing back inside to thaw before the fire.

One day Thomas returned from running an errand for the wife of a local fisherman with a crate containing four hens – Mozart, Schubert, Wagner and Bach. Upon release, the four feathered maestros scuttled angrily off to the coal shed where they would spend the rest of their days laying eggs as rich as velvet.

Thomas and Baxter would wrap up fruit and vegetables in

sheets of newspaper and hand them out to the townsfolk, occasionally throwing in the odd egg or jar of pickles, whenever they had surplus.

They worked around Baxter's school hours, tending the soil and sowing the seeds. The task was exhausting, but one that they grew to enjoy.

'It feels like we've raised a family,' Thomas said one evening to Baxter, as they sat together proudly observing the garden, their nail beds ridged with earth and their lips mercifully damp with wine straight from the bottle.

'Our proudest achievement to date,' Baxter said, taking a swig.

They ate Wagner for Christmas on their third year together.

Thomas did the deed, after Baxter spent a morning fretting over the prospect of losing one of his beloved quartet. He had resented the hens at first, but over time he had developed a fondness for the creatures that he tended as carefully as he did his garden.

They decorated the house for the season. War made these rituals seem both pointless and yet somehow more imperative. Wreaths of holly were hung like portholes in the doorways and long lays of coloured leaves and bound twigs were draped across the table and mantelpiece. In the drawing room stood a meagre tree heavy with baubles and trinkets bought years ago by Baxter's mother.

Peggy and Winnifred arrived as the clock struck eleven, dressed in their Sunday finest. Winnifred burst through the front door without knocking.

'Mr Baxter! Mr Thomas! Merry Christmas!'

She rushed towards them, arms wide. Her enthusiasm proved contagious, and soon even her hosts found themselves able to lay their concerns aside until morning. For one day, the war seemed to hold its breath and allow the spirit of the season to sing.

'Merry Christmas to you, my dear,' said Thomas, as Baxter took himself off to check on the roast. 'Do you feel confident that your behaviour this year has warranted a visit from Father Christmas?'

'Perfectly confident,' she said.

'I hope you like coal,' Peggy added, making her way towards Thomas as Winnifred followed Baxter towards the kitchen.

'Merry Christmas, music man,' said Peggy, kissing Thomas on the cheek as her mouth began to water at the succulent, salty smell which wafted from the kitchen. She could not remember the last time she'd had fresh meat, cooked slowly and with care.

Peggy dragged her sister home before bedtime.

'Another triumph, boys,' she said, waving farewell at the threshold.

Thomas and Baxter watched them walk off down the eerily quiet street.

'A funny child,' Thomas said, his hands resting on Baxter's shoulders as he directed him back inside to the armchairs either side of the tree. 'I think she'll go far.'

'Too far, no doubt,' Baxter said with a chuckle as he took the nearest glass and drained it of its contents.

Thomas topped up his drink and raised his glass.

'Merry Christmas, my love,' he said, handing Baxter a small parcel bound in newspaper and old string.

'But we said . . . I mean, thank you, but, Thomas I didn't . . .'

Thomas laughed and shook his head. 'It's nothing special. It isn't even new. So don't get too excited.'

Baxter teased the precious box in his hands.

'Open it then, stupid,' said Thomas, tapping Baxter's leg with his foot.

'I feel bad for having nothing to reciprocate with,' he said. 'This really is most unexpected.' Baxter untied the string with trembling fingers and carefully unwrapped the gift.

'Oh, Thomas,' he said. Inside was a silver pocket watch engraved by Thomas's father before he had died. Baxter picked it up and pressed it to his ear, the metal warm in his hands. He listened to the heartbeat of the second hand.

Thomas sipped at his drink and shook his head. 'It's not enough. Nothing ever could be. Promise me you'll keep it,' he said. 'I want you to have it.'

'But it's yours,' Baxter protested, overcome with emotion. 'It's so precious to you.'

'As are you. I know you will take good care of it.'

'I shall treasure it for ever,' Baxter said.

'And at least this way wherever I go, whatever happens to me, I know you'll keep me close to your heart.'

Baxter brought the watch from his ear, pressing it gently to his cheek, before examining it once more in the light of the fire and slipping it carefully into his breast pocket.

'You must always come back to me,' he said quietly. 'Wherever you go. You must promise me that you will always return. This is where you belong.'

Thomas rose from his chair and perched on Baxter's, wrapping his arms around him.

'I promise,' he said. 'I've nowhere else, for a start.'

Baxter burrowed his head into Thomas's chest.

'And what's more, there's nowhere I'd rather be than here, with you. I fear I'm no longer a whole on my own, Mr Baxter. Whether you realise it or not you've become my best half.'

18

Greg was surprised to find France a relief. The journey had taken no time, really. The train had entered darkness, and emerged in light, and that was that. There had been no fanfare, no perilous crossing. He merely felt a slight tingling in his buttocks from sitting down for too long, and a pressing urge to scrub his face with soap and water.

Despite the ease of their arrival, he felt an internal shift. He had never taken a journey further than a bus route would allow him. Nor had it ever occurred to him to do so. And yet he had woken that morning, left somewhere, and arrived somewhere new. It was as easy as that.

This new-found sense of possibility made him almost deliriously happy.

'That was so fucking easy,' he said giddily, over and over again, lugging the bags out of the station and onto the streets of Paris as Baxter hailed a taxi. 'I mean, properly easy,' he said, as thrilled and surprised if he were the first person ever to have realised how manageable the world really was. 'Look at that!' he yelled, pointing at a street performer dressed as a mime. 'Look!'

he said again, holding onto Baxter's arm as he pointed up at an elaborate building that spread to the skies like meringue. 'Baxter, you're missing it all,' he said, his eyes darting side to side with glee as the old man edged farther onto the road, until a passing cab slowed and stopped.

Baxter, of course, had seen it all before. His feet ached, his head throbbed and he yearned for the hotel and dinner; but despite all that, the boy's jubilant experience of *newness* – a long-expired thrill for the old man – was something he could not bring himself to dampen.

'It's like something off a film, isn't it?' Greg said excitedly, his eyes wide and wild, as if trying to physically wrap his senses around the entire city in one go, frightened that it might disappear before he got a chance to commit it fully to memory.

For the first time since they got there Baxter allowed himself a moment to take in the surroundings.

'Delightful, isn't it?' he said, placing his bag on the floor.

He could not remember the last time he had been somewhere that was new to him. And though the city was one he was more than familiar with, seeing Greg's delight fortified him enough to change course for a moment and wave the taxi onwards. 'Come on,' he said, picking up his bag and handing it to Greg. 'If memory serves there is a pleasant little café just around the corner. Let's sit down and take it all in before we make our way to the hotel. Might as well make the most of it while we're here,' he said, as Greg followed his lead.

'This is unreal,' Greg said, as they sat on wicker seats and were presented with menus by a waiter in a waistcoat. 'I mean, we were at home this morning. And now we're in another country, just sat down in a café like it's normal. But it's not. It's *mental*.'

Baxter made eyes at a waiter who came and placed a jug of water and two small glasses on the table.

'Home has its appeal, at times,' Baxter said, checking the menu.

'Depends on the home,' Greg added, trying desperately to summon the power of his B-grade GCSE French to make sense of the offerings.

'Now,' said Baxter, 'I want to go out for a nice dinner this evening but I suspect we should at least line our stomachs. What do you fancy?'

Greg shuffled in his seat, trying in vain to translate at least one word before him.

'Um ...' he said as the waiter tapped his pencil on the pad impatiently.

'Pancakes, do you like those?' Baxter asked and Greg nodded. 'Then we shall have crepes, and a drink.'

'Just a water for me thanks,' Greg said. Baxter's face twisted in horror.

'Nonsense! You're on your bloody holidays. Have a proper drink, man,' said Baxter.

Greg shrugged. 'A beer then I suppose, please,' he said as Baxter handed him the menu.

'Would you like to do the honours?' he asked and chuckled as Greg blanched at the prospect. 'Relax, relax,' he said, before turning to the waiter and launching into fluent French.

'*That*,' Greg said, when they were alone once more, 'was cool as fuck.'

Baxter shrugged, though Greg could tell the compliment had flattered the showman in him.

'Nothing that can't be learned with time and effort.'

Greg's nostrils pricked and he turned to the table behind then.

'What!' he said excitedly. 'You can smoke in here?'

Baxter nodded as their drinks arrived.

'Do you mind if I . . . ?' Greg asked, retrieving a packet from his backpack and a lighter from his pocket.

'Be my guest,' Baxter said. 'Though it's a filthy habit.'

'Yeah, I know,' Greg said, offering the packet. 'I hardly ever do it any more but we're on holiday, eh?'

'Quite,' Baxter said, reaching out and taking a cigarette.

Greg passed him the flame. 'Are you happy to be here then?'

Baxter made his way through his small glass of red and took another drag of his cigarette, exhaling a languid plume towards the ceiling.

How did he feel? His mood at that moment was impossible to articulate. 'Relieved,' he said eventually, certain that it was as close to accurate as he was going to get.

Thomas, though skilled with instruments, had always favoured songs with lyrics. Nothing pleased him more than a careful line or a tidy rhyme. Whenever he discovered a lyric that perfectly captured a feeling or image, he would play it over and over, fascinated and thrilled by the poetry.

Words were where he saw his truth.

Words were where he found his answers.

Baxter was never quite so certain. He could see the appeal of lyrics, but there was something about the fertile strangeness of sound without words that revealed more to him than a sentence ever could. Words had made him smart, novels had broadened his mind. Words showed him the world and its potential, but it was through sound that he learned how to feel it. No other medium could capture the illicit strangeness of *being* with quite such accuracy.

Given an instrument and a moment to ease his joints back into life, he could have played Gregory an answer. Yet with all his learning, with a vocabulary as rich as anyone's, he knew no words that could speak the language of his soul.

Greg looked at the old man askew. Baxter's attention had faded.

'You all right?' he asked.

As he spoke a waiter approached and placed two plates of sweet, fragrant crepes before them. The food seemed to snap Baxter's attention back to the here and now.

'That I am,' he said, placing his napkin across his knee. Greg copied his gesture, feeling a rare thrill of sophistication. 'I was just thinking,' said Baxter, 'that no matter how I feel, I know I've done the right thing.'

Baxter sliced a forkful of crepe, crowned it with a thick spoonful of Chantilly cream, and ate.

'Me too,' said Greg with gusto, folding his pancake in half with his fork and taking the entire thing in one sweet, gluey mouthful. 'Cheers, Baxter. I needed this more than I thought.'

Ramila sat perfecting her accent nail as Suzanne scrubbed away at a fresh new patch on the reception rug.

She had agreed to cover a double shift due to Greg's unexpected sabbatical – but not before she had secured a verbal guarantee of time and a half, two bank holidays off, employee of the month and a takeaway of her choice courtesy of petty cash. It was, she felt, a fair compromise.

'Time and time again,' Suzanne moaned, her knees bent and her arms working furiously into the stubborn stain with a damp scouring brush. 'It's the bloody paperboy, I'm telling you.' She flinched as her fingers began to spasm with what she feared were the first tremors of arthritis.

'I think it's Bobby,' Ramila said, making claws with her fingers and admiring her handiwork before crossing her arms and laying her head on the table. 'I saw him shoving Bourbons into his pockets earlier. One of them probably fell down his trouser leg.'

'You could at least offer to help,' Suzanne sighed, 'even if you've no intention of following through. The gesture wouldn't go amiss, you know?'

'I wish I could, Suzanne,' said Ramila blearily. 'But I'm too weak with exhaustion. It's this extra shift.' Her phone buzzed twice on the desk causing a straightening of her posture and a miraculous recovery.

'What have I told you about having phones out at work?' Suzanne barked, getting to her feet. 'If it's not the work phone I don't want to see it until break.'

'Oh this is brilliant,' Ramila said, ignoring Suzanne's gripes as she began replying to the message from Greg.

Guess Where We Are?

it said, along with a picture of a bicycle with a baguette in it.

PS. Please say sorry to Suzanne and tell her I'll make it up to her if she gives me the chance.

'Is that Gregory?' Suzanne demanded, snatching at the phone a fraction too slowly.

'Yes,' Ramila said, turning her back and texting with one hand as she swatted away Suzanne's extended arm.

'Tell him I want a word when he gets back,' she said. 'He's on a written warning for a start.'

Ramila finished her message.

Dear Greg and Baxter. I'm so pleased you're having a lovely time. Sadly, Ramila has died of heartbreak due to your treachery. I hope you are happy. The world has truly lost an angel. Lots of love, God Xx

PS bring me back 200 Lambert Menthols from Duty Free. I'll settle up on pay day.

'Look,' Ramila said, showing Suzanne the photo. Suzanne returned her glasses from the crown of her head to her nose and squinted at the miniscule image.

'Well, at least they're safe and well,' she said as a young man made his way through the front doors with a helmet under one arm and a takeaway delivery pouch under the other.

Suzanne frowned, beckoned him over and reached for the petty cash.

'I want that boy fit for when he gets back. I'm going to rip the little shit to shreds.'

She thrust a ten-pound note at the delivery man who, to his credit, didn't risk fishing for a tip.

Winnifred had stopped at the pub after aqua aerobics that lunchtime.

It had not been her intention to do so, but she was already in a funk when the first drops of rain landed on her head and the sight of the lettered glass proved too great a temptation. 'Courage' said the sign on the windowpane. *Well, bloody quite*, she had thought.

She missed Baxter terribly, and the feeling had been compounded by the email she had woken to that morning bearing news of his departure. She'd gone to her aerobics class hoping it would perk her up but the usual instructor had rung in sick and their replacement had not been up to much.

Still, two pints of bitter and a ploughman's lunch had brought her a certain comfort; and although the sherry she had taken in lieu of pudding (so as to not entirely undo the morning's efforts) sat heavily on her stomach, she was beginning to feel her spark return.

With that spark came an idea.

Yes, Baxter's mission was brave and important – no one knew better than she how much the pilgrimage must mean to him – yet she couldn't shake the sense that something was being overlooked. The more she thought about it the stronger she felt she had a part to play.

Baxter wanted Thomas's name remembered. But what of Baxter himself?

Baxter's story must be told.

And it was she who was to tell it.

'*THAT!*' Winnie looked up and saw a pretty girl pointing at her from a nearby table. 'That's the colour I want!' The two young men she sat with followed her glance and nodded in agreement.

Winnie was surprised by the attention. She tried to manoeuvre her wheels around a jutting barstool as the girl called over.

'Excuse me, love,' the girl said, though she couldn't have been much more than nineteen. 'Do you mind if I take a photo of your scooter thing? It's *exactly* the colour I want my hair.'

'Of course, dear,' Winnie had said, and slowly wheeled over to her table. 'My name is Winnifred, snap what you like.'

The girl excitedly retrieved her phone and began zooming in on the dark cherry of her machinery.

The group were on a free period from the local college. The free period had turned into a lunchtime excursion, which in turn had become an afternoon of tipsy truancy. The girl, Charlotte, had the dress sense of an undertaker and the eye-lashes of a Disney princess. It was a combination Winnifred found winning.

The boys were her gang, as it turned out. They were quieter but no less interesting. Their personalities came through in brief glimpses. After a good ten minutes they'd already started to relax – especially when they heard Winnie was on Twitter. The table had scrabbled for their phones as one, friending her in seconds flat.

'Oh my God, is that a rainbow sticker?' said one of the boys excitedly, glancing down at the rear wheel trim.

'That it is,' Winnie said proudly, sipping the sherry which the girl had bought her as thanks for her style inspiration.

'Oh my God, are you gay?' the girl asked, her hands pressed to her heart. '*Please say you are!*'

Winnie laughed and shook her head.

'Tried it once but it wasn't for me. Though I remain a keen ally,' she said, with her head bowed, 'as well you should.'

'As well we are,' said Charlotte, the mouthpiece of her trip-tych. 'I swear to God you are everything I want to be when I

193

grow up. You're fucking wonderful. Isn't she?' she said, brandishing her glass at the boys, who nodded enthusiastically.

'You're all sweet,' she said as she reversed an inch. 'I've been in a foul mood today. You have cheered me up no end but I really must go. I've a fireman coming this afternoon to check my alarms.'

'Oh no!' Charlotte said, her voice high with emotion. 'What's upset you?'

'A friend of mine is away,' Winnie said and the group moaned in drunken sympathy. 'Ninety-four years old and he's run away from his care home – to France if you can believe it. Anyway, I miss him.'

Winnie checked her purse for her house keys.

'Are you serious?' asked one of the boys. 'He sounds amazing. Please stay – you can tell us about him. *Please*,' he begged, as Winnie made her way around the bar.

'Tell you what,' Charlotte yelled across the room. 'Why not tweet your mate's adventure? We'll all retweet the shit out of it. You never know, you might become an Internet celebrity!'

And so she did.

19

Back at the hotel, they napped, showered and changed for dinner. Before leaving, they sat in their room, drinking champagne and smoking cigarettes by the balcony window.

Across the rooftops of Paris dusk began to draw in. It wasn't quite dark. Rather a different quality of light. Glowing neons and twinkling adornments made the evening seem like it had been painted by some drunken, joyous artist.

'It's so different here,' Greg said, mesmerised by the bustling street below. 'I mean I know it's only a city. I know bad stuff happens here too. But people here seem more alive, or happier? People ... *live*,' he said, as though the simplest of notions was alien to him.

'Life,' Baxter observed, twisting the stem of his glass between his fingers. 'It happens everywhere if you're open to it. You do sound like you're coming around to the continental way of things though.'

'I think I'm just coming around to the life part,' he said, watching a balcony in the distance. 'I like it here. Wouldn't live here though. I'm just pro anywhere that isn't home right now.'

'Anywhere is home if you make it so.'

'I won't move to France,' Greg declared after a long pause. 'Things are going to change though.'

'Very good,' said Baxter. 'But how so?'

Greg sighed and thought for a moment.

'Well, for one thing, I'm going to start making pancakes,' he said, as Baxter laughed.

'And drinking champagne, I hope.'

'Doubt it. Tastes like someone put turps in a SodaStream.'

'*Savage.*'

Somewhere in the distance an accordion pulled its first mournful notes, as Greg drained half his glass in one sharp glug.

'Snob.'

'To change,' said Baxter, tapping his glass against Greg's.

'To change,' said the boy.

'Looks expensive as hell, this, Baxter,' Greg whispered as they were shown to their table. 'I'd be fine with a sandwich back in the room, you know.'

'I bloody well wouldn't be,' Baxter said sternly, beckoning the maître d'. 'And anyway it's on me, so stop fretting about money. It's crass and joyless and I shan't have it.'

Greg sat down. He looked around at the cool elegance of the room and clientele and felt acutely embarrassed by his jeans and school-shoe combination.

'Only if you're sure. I feel like a right bellend though, dressed like this.'

'Then you need a drink!' Baxter declared happily, scanning the wine list. 'Everyone feels comfy with a drink in them.'

The meal came in instalments, like a poem sliced line by line.

Plate after plate arrived to the rapt joy of Baxter and the worried inspection of Greg, who prodded and sniffed each alien tower of nutrition before wolfing it down in one, keen not to seem ungrateful.

'Do I want to know what I just ate?' he asked, after a cold square of steak tartare had been taken in a single, panicked mouthful.

'Probably not,' Baxter said, his eyes closed as he savoured every last morsel. 'Did you enjoy it?'

'I'm pleased that I tried it,' Greg said, straining for the vaguest form of 'no' he could muster.

'That's the spirit,' he said. 'Shall we order another bottle?'

After dessert they sat quietly over half-glasses, as the establishment slowly drained of its custom.

'I enjoyed that, actually,' Greg said, feeling heavy with food and dizzy with drink. Around him the staff milled quietly and professionally, like ghosts who appeared only when willed. Baxter could have happily sat all night soaking in the ambience of the brasserie. Greg, however, sensed that they were the only thing separating the diligent waiters from a timely finish.

'You about ready?'

Baxter shook his head. 'Relax. Enjoy. Speak,' he demanded politely, and Greg felt that this was his inroad to the only conversation he'd wanted to have since the train journey.

'You going to show me those letters you've got stacked by your bed then?'

Baxter picked a petit four and popped it into his mouth, blooming with delight at the tiny explosion of sweetness. He handed the china plate to Greg, who accepted the treat – and declared it by far his favourite part of the meal.

'No,' he said, glancing at the ceiling. 'No,' he said again. 'I'll tell you about them though, if you'd care to listen?'

Greg nodded appreciatively. 'I'd love to,' he said, draining the last of the bottle into the old man's glass. 'Only if you want to though.'

Baxter pondered where to start.

'His name was Thomas,' he said, and paused. 'That is of upmost importance. You must promise me you will remember that, even long after I am gone.'

'I promise,' said Greg, feeling the plain name branded into his memory.

'Very well then,' Baxter said.

That first letter home had broken a spell of sadness which Baxter hoped would be the hardest thing he'd ever have to endure.

Life, he had always assumed, was a simpler game if played solo and maybe that was true. Yet ever since that summer's night when light rain had cooled hot dancers and the music man had tapped his door three times, Baxter had eschewed simplicity for the messy, volatile, multi-limbed existence of a duo. Life was less orderly as two – doubly so given their circumstances – but he adored it. He loved the constant, small surprises of a person you know better and more intimately than any other. It was that beautiful disarray he missed most when Thomas was taken.

The war had nearly passed them by when he was called up.

Tales of victory, sculpted from the loose wax of horror, were presented on the wireless and in print. The men were depleted. Even the ones who returned. Some spoke with pride of bravery and daring. Others simply slipped back into the nearest thing they could find to a normal routine, desperate to extinguish the ghosts they'd acquired during their time away. Many were injured, clean white gauze masking raw flesh and snapped bone. The two brothers who had taken over their father's cobblers shop had returned blind, deaf and entirely mute. Those who had kept their sight now stared at the world in horror – privy to some spirit realm visible only to the damned.

Willy Armstrong had returned home, kissed his mother hello, and excused himself for a walk. They found his clothes folded neatly next to his shoes at the far end of the pier, though the waves that had taken his body held it selfishly for three weeks, before belching forth his remains to the shock of a fisherman two ports south.

'You can't go,' Baxter had said over dinner that night. The letter sat like an open flame on the drinks cabinet, ready to conflagrate everything they had worked for over the preceding years.

The day had been long and unusually silent. Their words were infrequent and strained, as if each utterance gave unwanted credence to the reality of what they hoped was a bad dream. They had sat in the garden reading the same sentences over and over again. Staring at the words intently, desperate to become part of a world other than the one they were now living. Baxter cancelled their evening plans with Peggy and Winnifred and promised he would see Peggy the following day, alone.

'It's the law,' said Thomas, laying down his knife and fork onto a half-eaten plate of food. 'We all must do our bit.'

'I shall go instead of you,' said Baxter, and he meant it.

Thomas smiled and poured them each another glass of wine.

'They need you here,' he said gently. 'You're shaping the future we're fighting for.'

'How can you fight a war you don't believe in?'

'We fight for freedom. You believe in that, don't you?'

'I know, Thomas. But there are ways around it. You can tell them about us. They won't have you then.'

The prospect terrified him, but it was still marginally better than the alternative.

'And what then?' Thomas asked. Of course if the roles were reversed he'd be just as frantic for solutions. Of course he was frightened. But he did not want to let Baxter see any of it. 'We'd be arrested. It would be a different route to the same outcome – you and I apart. At least this way we can part with honour. I can do some good in your absence. I can help, I suppose,' he said.

At this Baxter found himself suddenly envious of whichever ravaged patch of the world would be blessed with the man that he wanted only to himself.

'You can't save them all,' he said, not entirely kindly.

Thomas smiled and reached across the table, taking Baxter's trembling hand in his.

'No,' he conceded, forcing the man to meet his gaze. 'But they must know that we tried.'

In the days that followed Baxter would soften in acceptance. The reality was that the world's needs outweighed his own, and no matter how desperate he was to alter history's onslaught – to haul some pipe askew, as to divert the insatiable deluge – it could not be done. Some wars cannot be won. And so they did their best to ignore Thomas's impending departure by living as they always had, only more urgently. Each drink savoured that moment longer. Each glance focused as if terrified they'd ever forget. Each kiss and every embrace, held.

As the day drew closer, small items were removed from their usual place ready to be packed. Clothes were held back from the wardrobe, folded and cornered and set aside until the time came. Night time became a terrain they both dreaded.

The night before the night before, they held an unofficial farewell at the house. Just Baxter, Thomas, Winnifred and Peggy.

The girls had baked a cake and brought pots of jam from their own personal reserves. Peggy had wrapped a box of soft tobacco from the shop and gifted it to Thomas, keen that he take as much luxury as she was able to afford. Winnifred had drawn a picture of a songbird the pair had spotted on one of their excursions along the jagged lip of the bay. Thomas was touched by Peggy's generosity. But the second gift came at him like an avalanche. His face burned with love as he looked down at the picture and the beaming child, so special to him he had no words for the place in his heart that she occupied. He had kissed Winnifred on the head and managed a tense *thank you*, before he excused himself to the hallway, where he hurriedly regained his composure.

Baxter had cooked as much as their rations would allow without leaving himself short for the rest of the week. It was a scant feast compared to former glories, but their stomachs were grateful and Baxter poured wine without thought for the future.

The air was warm and beyond the walls of the garden the sea lay flat and calm. The loveliness of the evening was such that Thomas, feeling the conversation veering towards the sentimental, declared it a waste to ignore it for a moment longer. They carried their glasses to the outdoor table, along with the cake and a bottle of port, to take in the last of the day before darkness fell.

On the lawn Thomas and Winnifred played a game which

largely involved her running at him with full force, bringing the pair to a tumbling play-fight on the grass.

Baxter and Peggy sat quietly and watched the boisterous game morph from one silliness to another. Winnifred pressed her palms firm into the ground and kicked up her legs, as Thomas caught her ankles and walked her forwards like a mower.

'Silly things,' Peggy said, finishing her port. 'She will be at a loss without him,' she added, sliding a firm hand onto Baxter's knee and giving it a squeeze.

'Yes,' he said, hypnotised by the game. 'It will take all that she has to cope.'

'Of course,' said Peggy, determinedly. 'And he'll be back in no time. Until then there are other lodgers, if the kitty requires it.'

'There are no others,' Baxter said, closing his eyes to disguise the tears.

'I am so, so sorry, my darling,' Peggy whispered. Baxter rubbed beneath his spectacles, blinking himself proper.

'Yes,' he said, for it was all he could manage, as Thomas and Winnifred bounded towards them in need of refreshments. 'As am I.'

Their own goodbye had been a shrouded affair. The secrecy they were used to – the notion of no tomorrow they were not.

They had woken early and risen late. The morning had been given to murmured recollections of shared moments, and slow, purposeful sex, before a more conventional hunger had forced them downstairs.

Baxter waited at the door as Thomas emerged with his bag packed, resplendent in uniform. Baxter handed him a letter.

'What's this?'

'To take with you,' Baxter said, staring to the floor.

Thomas tucked the letter into his top pocket and lifted his lover's face with two gentle hands.

'It's a map home,' he said as Thomas kissed his forehead.

'I found you once without a map, Mr Baxter. And I'll do it again, of that you can be certain.'

Baxter leant up and kissed Thomas once on the mouth as he felt himself beginning to cry.

'It's nowhere near everything I wanted to say, but it's as much as I could fit in a letter.' Thomas held him tight. 'Promise me you'll write,' Baxter said, removing himself from Thomas's embrace but keeping tight hold of his hands.

'At every opportunity,' he said, handing Baxter his tortoise-shell comb from his back pocket. 'Don't let standards slip when I'm gone, eh, old boy?'

Baxter took the comb and laughed.

'Look after yourself,' he whispered. 'For you belong to me now.'

'I always will,' Thomas added, one hand on the door. 'I do love you, Baxter,' he said, as the chill light of the day flooded their world.

'And I you,' Baxter said, watching Thomas leave for the very last time.

20

My Darling Baxter

How sweet it is to see your name held for ever in black ink. You have stopped me in my tracks already.

How I miss you, my love.

How I miss your face and your voice. The touch of your skin and the bend of your knee as you rise from bed to make tea. The way you shake your head as you hit a rare dud note on the piano. The way one loving glance can carry me higher than I ever imagined a person could.

I knew being apart would be hard. But I had not accounted for just how lacking I would be without you by my side. I suspect you have made me weak. Any strength I have will be spent making sure I return, so that we can be us once more. So that we can live the way we deserve to live . . .

Had Baxter known his first letter would arrive when it did, he'd have stopped time in anticipation of its arrival.

As it happened he had stretched out his day even longer than usual.

His initial instinct had been to let the loss devour him entirely. And yet in the weeks since Thomas had left he had managed to camouflage his sadness in the long reeds of routine. With Thomas's words ringing in his ears, he had made a brave effort to see that standards were indeed maintained. Each morning Baxter rose and readied, ate and worked, walked and read, slept and repeated. Even on weekends he was sure to plan a lengthy stroll or an outing with Peggy and Winnifred. His duties were such that he could, for vast swathes of the day, occupy his mind with tasks he usually thought frivolous.

He had stopped by the grocery shop on the way home from work that day. The sun was bright and the wind's subtle grip made itself known only to the more delicate patches of skin. Summer was ending, the light struggling to make it just another half hour, like a child determined to outlast its bedtime. He felt the season's shift in his very marrow.

Peggy had been a godsend during those first weeks. She knew well what was required of her. In the months after her parents died, she had relied on Baxter for so much. Without his support she would have struggled with the purse strings as well as her broken heart.

Seeing him enter the shop now, carrying a burden he had acquired through no fault of his own, caused her great pain. He was a proud man and a fine one, but behind his pressed suits and clipped manner lay a current of love so furious and powerful that she wondered how he managed to contain it – worried that one day he would no longer be able to. She knew Baxter could confide in her. She knew he would let her help. And she made it her mission never to let him down.

They shared tea at the counter, their conversation aimless and amiable and interrupted only by a last-minute customer. They discussed their respective days – the trials and challenges encountered in the run-up to lunchtime, the small instances of humour which made it all bearable. Winnifred's latest misadventures. Baxter's tales of the more spirited pupils in his class.

Eventually, though, Baxter knew he must face the evening alone again.

'A pleasure as always,' he said, retrieving his coat and kissing Peggy goodbye as she cleared the cups and saucers of their afternoon treat. 'My love to Winnifred,' he said, leaving the ping of the doorbell to fade in his absence.

Back home in the hallway he scooped the post from the mat, hung up his coat and re-adjusted a small crystal hedgehog so that it faced the sun of the drawing room, before sitting down at the kitchen table to make his way through the day's correspondence.

The sight of Thomas's handwriting made him gasp. His heart beat a rhythm that caused his nerves to blaze.

With a deep breath he gently prised open the envelope, retrieved the letter and began to read.

My Dearest Baxter . . .

He read and reread, passing his finger over each scratch and indent of the nib, imagining the hand on the pen.

After a fourth reading he pressed the envelope to his lips and slotted the note back inside.

'Be well, my love,' he whispered, breathing as though for the first time in a month, before retrieving his coat and hurrying back out into the cold air, to tell Peggy the news.

Baxter returned the letter carefully to its cover and laid it on the hotel bedside table. From his tidy collection he unwrapped the second, and lay it out on his bedspread. He had cared for the letters over the years as though they were living dependants. He had sought leather folders to protect them from the light. At stationers he had invested in costly slips to wrap each sheet individually, so they would not leech even the tiniest fragment of their contents.

But in the rock, paper, scissors game of life, time beats all he had found. And despite his diligence, the years had done their gradual work. Now a careless paw or overzealous crease would cause the fine paper to desiccate until the words were just dust in his hands.

Outside, the city's revellers made their way home from closing bars, as chairs were stacked and awnings pulled back. A city, he often felt, was most itself during those hours between the last bar closing and the first café opening. In his younger days he had relished walking alone through unfamiliar streets in those twilight hours. The odd sensation of an avenue he'd had to fight his way through just six hours prior now entirely his made him giddy. You notice more, on your own, he had found. Your senses become heightened by infinitesimal degree. Solitude was the key to true exploration – he had known this since childhood – and yet for all his self-containment, he would yearn for the absent other.

Greg dozed deeply and obliviously in the bed next to his.

'What do you think happened to him?' Greg had asked as

they walked home along the Seine much later that night. They leant on the concrete wall separating them from the water, staring out at the Eiffel Tower now peppered with light.

'Something bad,' Baxter said. Two tourists leant a dozen or so yards from where they stood and photographed themselves against the backdrop of the tower, as a man on a bicycle hawked wilting roses. 'I daresay I'll never know for sure. He's dead, of that I am certain, but it doesn't mean he shouldn't be remembered. It doesn't mean he should be denied his goodbye. Silly, really.'

'I think you're doing a good thing,' Greg said, finishing his cigarette, turning from the river and staring back at the dark boulevard. 'For both of you. I think you should be proud that you came. Even if you can't change what happened, I think you can change the way you feel about it. Make peace. If you can do that, well ... I reckon that's more than most people ever get to do. You should be proud that you're doing it. I'm proud of you.'

Back at the hotel, exhausted, they were relieved to find the comfort of their beds. Greg seemed to fall asleep almost as soon as he lay down.

'Sleep well, my boy.' Baxter took in the sight of the boy at peace. 'I could not have done this without you,' he said, even quieter.

'Baxter,' Greg mumbled, his eyes still shut. 'I just want you to know it'll be OK.'

'How so?'

'I just ...' Greg tried. 'I don't think you're being honest, that's all. I don't think you really wanted to come here to say goodbye. Not really.'

'Oh?' said Baxter, snuggling down until he was at one with the mattress.

'I think you've already said goodbye. When he went off you knew what might happen and I think ...' He struggled against the pull of sleep. 'I think you just wanted to make sure he wouldn't be forgotten. I think you wanted someone else to hear his story, and to remember him, and I think you wanted it to be me.'

'Well now ...' Baxter said.

'I just think you're scared it will have all been for nothing. But it wasn't. Because I know now so you don't have to worry. Neither of you will be forgotten. Neither of you will disappear when you die.'

Baxter smiled, as Greg let out a small laugh and curled into a tight ball.

'I see you, Baxter. I see you like you saw me. You care but you're scared to let it show, and I know you'd never ask. So I just wanted you to know that I'll remember for you. I'll tell your story and I'll tell his. And I'll tell mine. I won't let myself live quietly in the dark any more. That's my gift to you.'

The old man and the boy fell asleep.

Both feeling lighter than they had done in some time.

Each wearing a smile.

My Darling Baxter

It seems that I have indeed brought a piece of our world along with me. Alas not the piece I'd have hoped, for our friend from the coal shed, a certain Jack Bletch Esq., occupies the bottom bunk three beds down from mine.

You will be pleased to hear that the war has yet to dull

his entrepreneurial spirit, nor sharpen his soft edges. In fact, as we speak he has acquired a dashing purple eye for his attempted theft of General Goodwill's final cigarettes. Whether or not his actions reach the stern arm of court martial is yet to be decided. All I can say is that his vision, or lack thereof, will spare the lives of at least one of our friends on the other side. Though even with his faculties intact he poses minimal threat, it has to be said.

What a small world it is after all. And yet, with an ocean between us, how cruelly enormous it seems . . .

Thomas sat in his bunk, oblivious to the dull hum of activity around him.

Dropped from the skies and birthed from the sea, they had trudged across the soft sand for miles before arriving at base camp. With their beds allocated and their introductions made, the men had gone silently to bed that night; the sound of machines booming death on some unseen patch echoing in the distance.

Those unable to control themselves had done their best to silence their sobs as the first darkness of battle engulfed them. Those who managed to hold back had had the good grace not to mention it over breakfast the next morning, as the red-eyed and the dead-eyed focused on the meagre rations, intently ignoring the screams from the medical tent.

The air was wet like the ground. It was a moisture that soaked to the bone and stayed there, like an infection untreated. The camp was gripped by a palpable tension as they awaited their orders. The men with whom Thomas shared his final days – the wounded as well as the waiting – made fast friends at arm's length. Keen for human connection, but wary lest their kinship end abruptly. To mourn was a luxury the men and the boys could ill afford.

Jack spotted Thomas on that first afternoon. He approached with caution. Thomas's easy manner and propensity with the banjo marked him out as the entertainment for the men whose spirits had yet to be crushed. His abundance of tobacco, too, and his readiness to share, cast him as a rare and valuable ally for the troops.

'Good day,' said Thomas, suppressing his surprise.

'I thought you only fought wars over coal,' said Jack with a sneer. He had avoided both Thomas and Baxter since that first altercation all those years ago. Yet still felt a tingling recollection of shame at being struck down so decisively.

'Private Bletch,' Thomas tried once more, and nodded once in lieu of a handshake. 'I take it you're well.'

'Very,' he had said. 'No other half today?' he said, glancing around elaborately, though he knew Baxter's job had kept him on the home front.

'I come alone, and in peace,' said Thomas, extending his hand to Jack's though it pained him to do so.

'If you're after a friend then you're mistaken,' Jack said, as a group of older men surrounded them and began cajoling Thomas towards a game of cards.

'We're all friends here, Jack,' Thomas said, as he was led away. 'Brothers in arms, my friend. Brothers in arms.'

Still waiting for his orders, Thomas had spent his day waiting, waiting and trying to thaw by the fire. He had watched trucks arrive and unload the agonised fragments of men, stretchered away to face suture and scalpel.

The prospect of battle terrified him but he suspected the anticipation was just as bad in the long run. His nerves played notes in the upper register that reverberated throughout his entire body. The boredom he could handle. Even the cold could be ignored for stretches of time.

But the waiting was agony.

The only saving grace was the fact that without his pocket watch he had no concept of time and was unable to watch the hours pass by in molten anguish.

My Darling Thomas ... he read in bed that evening.

The letter was all he had of Baxter, in a tangible sense. His mind was filled only with thoughts of him. He spent his nights aching for the curve of his back to warm his outstretched hand, wishing to be woken by the melody of his whisper.

He knew the letter by heart, and yet time and time again he was drawn to the physical thing – holding it in his hand gave him such comfort, as if touching paper were touching souls.

His moment of tranquillity was interrupted only when Private Lyle popped his head into the tent, his knee jerking with excitement.

'Thomas,' he whispered. 'Come quick, we're playing pontoon.'

At first he resisted, though was worn down by the young man's insistence.

'Very well,' said Thomas, and rose wearily, slipping the letter tightly back into the cigarette tin beneath his pillow. 'But just the one. Tonight my mind is somewhere else.'

'Oh yeah?' asked Lyle. He had overcome, Thomas could tell,

a stammer in his youth. But the lingering uncertainty of his own voice still haunted him to this day. And so when he spoke he did so in quick, spitfire sentences, as if scared to slow down lest he never start up again. 'You got a sweetheart at home?' he asked, each word a clipped, friendly bullet, patting Thomas on the back as they made their way towards the game.

21

They shared a cigarette in silence as the taxi pulled away, leaving them alone at the entrance of the memorial.

They had risen later than intended. Baxter had readied, changed ties, and then the entire suit, before finally settling on something he felt suitable for the day.

'Bloody French water,' he mumbled at the mirror as he fiddled with an invisible kink in his hair.

'There's nothing wrong with the water,' Greg said from the bed where he sat. 'There's nothing wrong with your hair. You look nice.'

'Yes, well, at least that makes one of us,' Baxter said, glancing at the boy, whose ankle socks prodded a good three inches from the hem of his trousers.

Greg had taken advantage of the bathroom first that morning. He had washed and brushed and sprayed and combed four damp fingers through his hair to rid it of static. Having had no idea of what their journey would entail – and a fair certainty, up to the point of departure, that he would bail at the last minute – his packing had been erratic and ill-conceived to say the least. He had jammed into his rucksack a pair of jeans, three changes of underwear, a short-sleeved shirt, two T-shirts, some swimming trunks and a cagoule. He had emerged from the bathroom to find Baxter sitting alone with his head in his hands, deep in thought.

'You doing all right?' Greg asked gently, aware now of a fraction of the poignancy the day held for the old man. He placed a hand gently on his shoulder as he passed him by to hang his towel on the radiator beneath the window.

Baxter was roused and raised his head.

'Absolutely bloody not,' he barked, taking in Greg's outfit. 'Change!' he demanded, pointing back to the bathroom.

Greg glanced down at himself and then back up at the man, whose eyes were red and who looked truly old for the first time since he'd met him.

'Don't be tight, Baxter,' he objected, genuinely wounded. 'This was expensive, this.'

'Not suitable for a day like today. You shall wear a suit.'

'I've not got a suit. I chucked out the one I got for our Michael's funeral that night. Was only from the supermarket anyway. It looked shit. I don't see what all the fuss is about.'

Baxter's jaw hung agape as he shook his head.

'Non-negotiable. We haven't time to head out and buy you a new one. You shall have to adopt one of my cast-offs for the afternoon.'

'I'll never fit into them.'

Baxter looked at the suits he'd hung out on the wardrobe door and then at Greg before shrugging as he stood up.

'Breathe in deep, my boy. Because you're not leaving this

room until you're respectable,' he said, and made his way to the bathroom.

Greg walked to the far end of the car park to dispose of the cigarette butt properly, before he made his way back towards where Baxter stood by the church.

The day was warm but overcast. One or two cars sat at far ends of the stretch of gravel beside the entrance, but they were more or less alone, which felt good and right.

The silence from inside was a tidy, respectful quiet. Its chilly nothingness reminded Greg of the church he had returned to as Michael's wake at the rugby club came to a drunken slump. He had been surprised to find the doors ajar, and sat alone on a pew amongst the iconography, watching the sun darken the stained-glass saints. Untroubled by religion and previously unconcerned with this fact, he had nonetheless found himself yearning for an answer, for some meaning to emerge from the church's garlands and trimmings.

None had come. He had left after dark, his heart as heavy as when he had arrived. His uncertainty was as staunch then as it had been since two police officers had knocked on his door one chilly afternoon. And yet the silence and solitude had helped, in its own small way. The pin-drop hush had allowed him to hear his own thoughts clearly, even if he was yet to make sense of them. Acceptance would be a long time in coming, if ever it did.

'You all right, Baxter?' he asked as two decorated veterans made their way from the war memorial and back towards their car. Baxter did not reply. 'Not being funny, right, but I don't reckon you're getting this suit back. I think it's tattooed onto my skin or something. It fucking *knacks*. And I look a right tit in it, too.'

Baxter looked up slowly at the boy. The sun shone in his eyes and the pull of his lover's farewell was becoming difficult to ignore, though he was not quite ready.

Greg, he had noticed, wore the suit in the same way that he wore his adulthood – with strained perplexity and great discomfort. And yet he could not help but smile at the efforts he had made; the huge boy in the ridiculous suit with the rough mouth and the kind heart.

'You look like a fine young man,' Baxter said, shuffling on the spot as he gripped at his cane tighter, ready to begin his journey. 'I shall be very proud to be seen with you, Gregory.'

'Me too,' he said, linking Baxter by the arm. 'You ready to go inside?' he asked, and the old man nodded. 'Also, what exactly is it we do once we're in there?'

'We remember,' he said. 'And we say goodbye.'

'Come on then,' Greg said, initiating the slow walk. 'Let's show them how it's done.'

Winnifred sat on the salon chair staring at her reflection in the mirror's harsh lights.

'You're a babe all right,' Aisha conceded, resting her hands on Winnie's shoulders as she looked at the old woman who had been frequenting her hairdresser's on and off for the last three years. 'What's it to be then?'

Winnifred sighed.

'Something special, today. A real burst of glamour. I've found myself quite in demand,' she said proudly.

Since sending that first tweet, Winnie's life had felt like a celebrity whirlwind, albeit from the confines of a fleece cardigan in a Tyneside bungalow.

Let me tell you a story, about a man I knew, and a man I know, she had begun.

It starts many years ago, and has no ending – at least not yet. But you may find it interesting, if you've the patience, she continued.

Immediately the gang from the pub retweeted her, and then another stranger and another.

And so she continued, well into the night. Beginning with Baxter and ending in France. A love story in instalments. Her first true masterpiece had been written in just one night, and she'd barely broken a sweat.

The tale, however, had gained momentum somewhere in the ether. More and more unknown faces took on the story and relayed it to their followers. It even became a bit of local news and now, freshly coiffed by Aisha and having rubbed the best part of a tub of cold cream into her face in anticipation, she sat and waited for the reporter to arrive.

With her nails filed and freshly painted, Winnifred arranged the treasures on her coffee table. There were letters from Baxter to Peggy during his wilderness years after the war. There was a photograph, so faded it had all but disappeared, of Thomas leading Winnifred across the beach on a summer's day. An old ration book she'd found when she had sold the shop once and for all, and could not bring herself to discard. A hairclip of her sister's and a picture of her and Baxter, resplendent and young. And most treasured of all, a photo of the two men, lying side by side in the sand. Thomas's head had dipped and his dark eyes were tired after a day chasing her around. Baxter looked straight at the camera, his eyes full of contentment and his mouth fixed into the same, wide smile he always wore in Thomas's company. Their supine bodies did not quite touch and yet if you looked closely you could see Thomas's caring hand at an angle in the sand, teasing its way towards his beloved.

She had also dug out one or two mementoes of her own. Not entirely relevant to the story, but testament to her character and pertinent, she felt, to her own role in it all.

There was her first wage slip from the accountant's firm, pasted proudly into a diary. There was a Christmas card from her sister which she had carried with her everywhere in the months after her death. There was a photograph, too, taken by a lover in Malta some years after the war. The gentleman whose name she could not recall had snapped her naked, save a white blanket covering her from the waist down, her breasts bare against the bed sheets, her face bathed in light from open balcony doors.

'What a bloody babe,' Winnie said, nodding at the photograph as she shoved a mouthful of crisps into her mouth.

'I've no real food in to give you,' she had told the young reporter on the phone when she'd rang to arrange their interview. 'But I've loads of wine, so we'll be fine. I can always ring us a takeaway if we get the munchies.'

The woman had laughed and informed her that a cup of tea would suffice. Winnifred, in turn, had told her to stop being such a stick in the mud. The reporter had become fascinated with the love story that had gone untold until now. A love story that, it turned out, had taken place not two streets back from where her grandparents now lived. She was honoured, she said again, that she would be the one to tell it.

'You're the one who types it,' Winnie had corrected her with a smile. 'This is our story. You just make sure you get it right. And be kind, my dear.'

Suzanne was updating the message board. She had received news that Greg and Baxter were soon to return via the medium of Ramila's texts with Greg. She was still furious with them. She had also missed them. And had taken it upon herself to make a 'Missing' poster which she plastered all round Melrose Gardens, so as to embarrass them, confront them *and* make them smile the moment they walked through the doors.

Ramila was on the phone. 'Yes, yes, yes. Absolutely. No, I agree. Whenever is good for you.'

Ramila removed the receiver from her ear, muffling it against her shoulder and omitted a long, soft squeal of excitement.

'*It's happening*,' she whispered to herself, '*it's finally happening . . .*'

'I do not like the sound of this,' Suzanne said.

'I can't wait to talk to you. Me and him go way back,' she said.

'Ramila,' Suzanne warned, returning to the desk.

'Oh, that won't be a problem either, I will sort it out, I mean, I am *practically* his daughter.'

Ramila thanked her correspondent, cementing their meeting for later that afternoon.

'Do I even want to know?' Suzanne asked, checking the coast was clear before taking a blast of her vape – a new addition to her routine, but a necessary one since Baxter's flit had left her nerves in ribbons.

Ramila breathed deeply and nodded.

'Suzanne, you know how much I do for you and this place,'

she said, raising her hand politely against the anticipated intervention from her boss. 'Well, it's finally time I asked you for something in return.'

Suzanne feigned indifference as she tapped a pen across the to-do list she had made for herself that morning.

'I need two hours off,' said Ramila.

Suzanne guffawed. 'And what, *exactly*, is so urgent?'

Ramila began packing her belongings into her handbag.

'Hair and make-up,' she said, her face contorted into a look of pleading desperation. 'A reporter's coming around later to talk to us all about Mr Baxter, but she's mainly coming to talk to me seeing as I am his closest confidante here.'

Suzanne choked on a lungful of Strawberry Cheesecake eSmoke.

'Look, ever since Winnie started live-tweeting Baxter's life story, everyone's on about him. He's famous!'

She handed her mobile to a puzzled-looking Suzanne.

'Here, just scroll down Winnie's timeline. Anyway, the papers are doing a story about him and his boyfriend from years ago. This really could be my big break.'

Suzanne took the phone with one hand, took a vape, and wished to God she'd stuck with Marlboro Red.

Thomas's unit drove back from their first day of battle while the evening was still light. Fewer returned than had left that morning. They were largely silent.

The men in the truck behind them sang songs celebrating king and country. The men in the truck in front were the grievously injured, praying merely to survive the journey back to camp.

Thomas stared at the floor. He could not bear to look at any one of his comrades. Not after what they had witnessed that day.

He had survived. But so, too, had he killed. And something inside him had shifted irrevocably. Even amid the chaos and frenzy of battle, the field around him had silenced the moment he had a direct hit.

The world he had seen that day did not exist in the world he had known before. The noise was too loud. The horror was too succinct. *How*, he thought as they disembarked at camp, *could a world so full of love be privy to such vast and unyielding hatred?*

'Thomas,' said Private Johnston, greeting him from the bus as the men who were able to walk were quietly absorbed by the crowds. 'Come and have a song with us.'

Thomas declined and made his way towards his tent.

'Later then,' he yelled after him. 'You owe us a tune.'

Thomas waved without looking back.

He finished a cigarette outside the tent and breathed deeply, staring up at the sky. What time was it, he wondered. Four? Five? The battle had felt both dizzyingly fast and agonisingly slow. Would Baxter be home from work, perhaps sharing tea with Peggy in the shop, maybe tending to the day's correspondence over a glass of something sweet?

He smiled at the thought, flicked away the butt and made his way inside.

The moment he saw him he froze.

'What on earth are you doing?' he said.

Jack was standing by Thomas's cot. As he turned, he hurriedly slipped something down the front of his trousers.

'Come back here at once,' he demanded, as the boy fled through the tent's rear entrance.

22

Baxter and Greg walked quietly through the pathways that ran between the neatly kept lawns and the alabaster headstones.

'So many without names,' Baxter noted as they came to a stop; two black beetles in a sea of white, staring out at the respectful order which iced the horror beneath.

Baxter bowed his head and Greg did the same. Their eyes were drawn to the crisp clarity of the immaculate rows. Memories bleached and ordered. Each man was pulled inwards in that moment, their mind's eye trained on the vanishing point: the moment where the one they had loved the most was gone.

The graveyard was empty save for them. Greg's suit pulled tighter at his raw skin in the warm air, yet he had grown accustomed to the discomfort. He stood as straight and proud as the fabric would allow him, his arm gently pressing against Baxter's, as they observed the anonymous sea of white rolling out before them.

'Do you think he's here?' he asked, as Baxter raised his head to the sun.

'My investigations implied that this is the only place he

could be. And I think that he is, as much as anybody can know these things.'

'Like you can feel him?'

'I don't believe in an afterlife of any sort, Gregory. Not in the traditional sense. Not in any sense, really.'

'Me neither,' said Greg, bending his knees to observe one of the named gravestones. 'Do you think it would be easier if we did?'

'No. Not really. Though that's not to say I don't believe in anything.'

'Yeah? What's your religion then?'

'A hodgepodge of morals and stances, bound by ritual and routine. No different to anybody else, I suppose. I believe in life, Greg. I believe in life that is lived and I believe in the time that we have when we are here. I believe life marks you as much as you do it, and the key is to learn from the scars that you bear, and those which you leave in turn.' He dipped his head to gaze as clearly as he could at the whitewashed stone. 'It seems so unfair though, doesn't it?'

'What does?'

'All these stories, all these boys. Most of them without a name. They didn't deserve it. How can a life just be forgotten? Erased for eternity as though it never happened?' he asked, a tear forming in his eye. 'Somebody's child, brother. Lover.'

'You can't save them all, Mr Baxter,' Greg said, linking his arm through the old man's.

'No,' Baxter said, nodding once towards the graves beyond. 'No,' he said again. 'But they must know that we tried.'

'Shall we say goodbye?' Greg asked eventually, turning back to the grand memorial, where pale colonnades held the names of the known dead.

Baxter stood proud and nodded, turning on his heels.

'I think so,' he said eventually. 'It's time.'

Night was drawing in as Thomas made his way through the tent, following Jack out into the evening.

The cawing of gulls yearned across the water's edge. All around, men shared jokes and took turns on damp cigarettes, plucking familiar songs from filthy, tuneless strings.

The scent of cooking wafted from the camp's kitchens. Parched throats swallowed saliva. Emtpy stomachs rumbled. The promise of food was the common focus. Thomas had a hearty appetite, but could not bring himself to care. He could live with whatever was left when dinner was over – he was not so certain he could survive without what Jack had taken from him.

'Have you noticed Private Bletch?' he asked, skipping across the tent ropes and making his way to a group of men who seemed oblivious to his frenzy.

'Has anyone what?' said one, his attentions focused keenly on the word game was he playing.

'I think he went that way?' said another, pointing towards the far edge of camp. 'Though I couldn't be certain. Why, what's he done now?'

'He has taken something of mine, and I want it back,' said Thomas, making his way in the direction suggested by the boy. 'If you see him make sure you keep him here.'

Thomas frantically searched the grounds.

Jack had relieved Thomas of his belongings. A fortnight's worth of tobacco – if measured with care – had been pilfered from his box. The picture drawn by Winnifred had been torn in haste and left in pieces on his blanket. That was not all. Baxter's letter was gone too.

The words that he had lived for during his time at war.

The words that were evidence of the life he held dear.

The words that could damn him as easily as they had heartened him.

The general's tent sat at the edge of camp. It was round, like a decorative coin, and its roof pitched at the tip. A flag hung limp on the gentle wind. The troops largely steered clear of the vicinity, and that evening was no exception. Mostly they were concerned that an uttered obscenity or some flash of frivolity would catch the general's attention and result in punishment. Thomas had little experience of the general personally, but what he had seen – and heard – had not entirely warmed him to the man. He had a staunch manner of an individual who'd had to cauterise emotion in order to make the decisions required of his role. And yet, as tin clanked metal and the last boys were called to the mess, he saw no other option but to seek his help.

'Permission to enter, General,' Thomas said from the doorway, his face warmed by the oil lamp that was lit within.

'Permission granted,' came the reply, and he stepped inside.

Beside the general's desk stood Jack, his eyes to the ground, his chest heaving from his hasty escape. Thomas's belongings were nowhere to be seen.

Thomas greeted the general and stood in salute for longer than was usually required, the silence of the room crisp and certain.

'At ease, soldier,' the general conceded eventually, as Thomas's body relaxed as best it could.

'I'm here to report a crime,' Thomas said, as Jack's eyes met his, and the faint glimmer of a smirk faded like dusk.

'Private dismissed,' the general ordered, as Jack saluted once and made his way from the tent.

'I'm afraid my news pertains specifically to Private Bletch,' Thomas insisted, as Jack glanced back only to be nodded on by the general. 'He has been stealing from the men,' he said, taking a step towards the desk just as Jack closed the tent flap behind him and the general spread his hands on the desk, framing Baxter's letter.

'We should have brought flowers,' Baxter lamented as they stood together, staring up at the memorial. At the arches, poppy wreaths lay at strange angles. Letters in sealed envelopes had been slipped carefully amongst the gaps, and fingerprints faded on the names carved low enough on the stone for visitors to touch.

'No point,' Greg said. He was struck dumb by the colossal fact of the memorial, and its sheer beauty up close. 'They'd only die.'

Baxter laughed. 'True, but they're poignant while they last.'

'Aren't we all,' Greg said. '*Hopefully*,' he added, as Baxter nodded.

'Do you ever lay flowers for Michael?'

Greg shook his head. 'Never visit. I sometimes have a cigarette where he died though, the way we used to when he was alive.'

'A sacrifice in smoke. A true Viking funeral.'

'Fit for a king,' Greg whispered, as Baxter rummaged in his inside pocket and retrieved a pocket watch.

'Here,' he said, handing over the object that had warmed against his chest all day. 'He may not be etched in stone, but his name should be here in some manner.'

Greg took the watch and awaited instruction.

'Find a soft patch of earth and press it down as far as you can. I suspect it shall be exhumed sooner rather than later but . . .' he trailed off.

'Wait there,' Greg said, stepping to the edge of the monument, where marble met earth.

He pressed his fingers into the earth with difficulty at first. The ground had not been as forgiving as he would have liked. But once the initial work was done the rest came easily. The watch pressed slowly into the mud, swallowed inch by inch, until it was all but gone.

'There you go, Thomas,' Greg said, quietly pressing until the watch was one with the monument. 'This will do you for now.'

'The letter makes for interesting reading,' said the general, standing slowly from behind his desk.

Thomas swallowed hard.

'May I please have my letter back,' he asked, as the general looked down at the note, and up once more at the man who stood unapologetic before him.

'No,' he said quietly, picking it up and passing the words across the lip of the oil lamp, causing ashes to dance up to the ceiling of the tent like fireflies. Within seconds of the letter's destruction Baxter's words surrounded them in smoke. Thomas felt the act of cruelty cut like a blade. 'And let me be perfectly clear. Whilst on duty nothing is yours, Private Cohen. Not one thing. You live by the grace of God. You'd do well to remember that. Now, what have you to say for yourself?'

'I am the victim of a theft. The defence is not mine to make,' he said, as the general nipped the final embers between the tips of his fingers.

'Am I to believe what Private Bletch has relayed to me this evening?'

'I wouldn't know, sir. I was not fortunate enough to catch his tale.'

'That the letter was written by a Mr Baxter? And that you and this Mr Baxter . . . cohabit?'

Thomas smiled and closed his eyes before opening them again slowly, as if waking from a bad dream.

'Yes, sir,' he said, as the general fumed.

'Completely unrepentant,' he said, his head shaking gently in exasperation. 'And that you offered your goods to Private Bletch in exchange for the chance to observe him . . . debasing himself?'

Thomas grew red with fury.

'This is a downright lie, sir,' he said.

The general nodded, as if pleased to have proved his own theory. 'So not entirely without defence, then?'

'Facts are facts. I shall apologise for any wrongdoings and nothing else. I never once acted inappropriately with Private Bletch.'

'And yet your relations with this Baxter . . .'

'I shan't apologise,' Thomas said, as the oil lamp between them flickered. 'I've done nothing wrong.'

'It is a crime.'

'On paper,' Thomas objected.

'In practice,' he hissed. 'How can I rest safe knowing this exists amongst my troops?'

'It exists only in the letter you just burned.'

'It isn't safe for the men. I must consider them,' he said as Thomas couldn't help but smile.

'The men's safety is your concern?' he asked, not entirely seriously.

'Primary,' the general said curtly.

'I can assure you I pose no threat.'

'You can make no such assurance, though you could at very least show some trace of remorse. Have you no shame, Private? Have you no regrets?'

Thomas had been removed from all that he loved.

At that point there was little chance of return.

All he had left was his truth.

And so he clung to it with all the determination he could muster.

'None,' he said. 'None whatsoever.'

Outside the dining tent Jack eased his pace and looked out at the sea. The evening cooled against his face, as in the distance horizon formed the impenetrable seal separating him from his home. The sound of the men eating and talking seemed to echo through the camp, the tuneless beat of metal on metal, the rapt cheers and the bustle of bodies cajoling for seconds. Though his stomach cried out, he hesitated a moment longer. He removed the tin discreetly from where he had lodged it uncomfortably beneath the waistband of his trousers. He picked out a half-smoked cigarette and returned the stash to his pocket.

'Your predicament is troublesome to me. But your lack of repentance leaves me lost for words. If anything, it is the greater crime,' the general said quietly.

'Love is no crime,' said Thomas. The general's eyes widened. He was certain now that only one option remained.

'You do not know love,' he said. 'What you know is wrong.'

'Then I don't want to be right.'

'Think very carefully now, Private. Is your honour that important to you?'

Thomas grew heavy with the weight of the day.

'Not mine,' he said. 'But his? Yes.'

'How can you stand there and defend what you've done? What you are? The letter was an affront to all things decent.'

'With all due respect, sir. Everything I'm fighting for was in that letter.'

Their eyes locked. The general felt undefeated by their exchange and yet his inability to break the man, or rather the man's stubborn refusal to let himself be broken, made him furious. He felt anger bloom inside him like molten glass blown into an ugly, half-formed shape.

'Private dismissed.'

Thomas saluted once and turned to exit the tent, before he could notice the general remove a pistol from beneath his uniform.

Jack heard the single gunshot cut through the night. Its echo paused time. He felt a tremor rip through his bloodstream. With a trembling hand he placed the half-finished cigarette between pursed lips, teasing its edge with the flame of a match that fought hard against the wind, before losing its battle against the unyielding elements, and flickering to darkness in his hands.

'Why is it so hard?' Greg whispered, as he and Baxter stood side by side, lost in memory.

Baxter's mind remained half in the past, yet he found himself able to answer the boy's questions with the only real lesson he had taken from a long and full life.

'It's kindness,' he said, as Greg turned to look at him. 'That's what's so hard. That the first lesson we are taught is the first we forget. And yet were it for kindness, maybe life could simply be enjoyed, instead of endured and examined retrospectively. That sort of kindness is easy and yet so painfully elusive. But it's there. And it's so, so obvious . . .'

Greg thought for a moment and wiped a tear from his eye.

'Maybe you're right,' he said.

'Oh, but I am.' Baxter nodded.

'Does it get easier?' Greg asked, as they stared down at the patch of earth in which Thomas's name was now buried.

'No. You just get better at it. Such is life,' said Baxter, wrapping an arm around Greg's waist as the boy leant in to him, uneasily at first, but gradually relaxing, until he was comfortable enough to allow him to shoulder just a fraction of his weight. 'We think that it is the absence that hurts the most, but it isn't. It's the love that remains; the weight we inherit to carry alone. But in time . . . in time the agony becomes exquisite, in its own way, born as it was of happiness. We're lucky, you and I. Despite our yearnings. We've known a pure form of what most people only see a fraction of and we must never forget it. We must remember, always, but most of all we must live. Gregory, listen to me. Live your life, live it bravely and beautifully. That is the greatest tribute you can pay to all to those who could not.'

They were quiet again, as above them the birds found their voices and began calling a gentle song.

'Promise me you meant what you said. That you'll remember his name,' Baxter said as he gathered himself. 'Long after I'm gone. Promise me you'll remember. And you'll tell it to anybody that will listen.'

234

At first the music was formless and gauche. Notes bumped into one another and the whole thing hung awkwardly. But somewhere in amongst the mess of it, Baxter could hear a melody. Tentative as it was, it shimmered nonetheless, hovering and dipping as loosely as cigarette smoke in the air. One had to focus to hear it. Try too hard and it slipped from your grasp. But if you sat back and closed your eyes, as Baxter did in that moment, it was there. The melody began to emerge from the chorus, as the conductor curated and summoned forth the sublime from the ridiculous.

The children found their rhythm, and Baxter smiled as he let the music take over him.

23

Upon hearing of Baxter's return from Suzanne, Winnifred arranged a lift to the station with Ramila to welcome the pair home.

After charging five pounds apiece for petrol money, Ramila hauled Winnifred's scooter from the boot of her car and scanned the vicinity for the closest pub.

'I'm not paying you for today, mind,' Suzanne said, getting in the first round at the station bar as the old girl and the young woman bonded over their mutual love of a vulgar anecdote. 'And steady on!' she demanded, sitting down as the pair gulped at their drinks. 'I can see what's going to happen. You're going to get rat-arsed before they've even left Durham and I'm going to have to stump up the taxi fare back,' she said, lowering Ramila's drink from her lips and placing an optimistic beer mat over the rim of her glass.

'Quite right too!' Winnifred said, unfazed by Suzanne's authority but increasingly fond of the woman all the same. She had a good heart hidden well by a stern voice and a ready temper. That, combined with her red hair and pleasing bust, reminded her fondly of her own sister. 'Let the girl have some fun. We're women of the world, you and I, Suzanne. We can always find our own way home.'

'Easy for you to say, on your bloody wheels. And speaking of which we've still to talk about the whopping great dent you left in my reception desk. Don't think I've forgotten about it.'

Suzanne took two sips of her own gin and tonic as Winnifred gave an innocent shrug.

'Excuse me, but do I know you?' asked a well-dressed woman on the way past their seats towards the train toilets.

'Unlikely,' Baxter said to the lady. 'But travel safe nonetheless, my dear.'

It was not the first time Greg had noticed people taking more of an interest in them than was entirely necessary. There had been tapped shoulders and whispering and lengthy stares. He always felt, to a degree, as though he were being scrutinised. Usually he chalked it up to self-consciousness and neurosis, but today he was certain it was rooted in objective fact. He and Baxter were getting noticed, commented upon and even – as they had made their way through King's Cross towards the platform for the Newcastle train – photographed by surreptitiously poised camera phones.

'I think she fancied you,' Greg said, taking a sip of his beer as the train entered Northallerton and an announcement was made as to their next stop.

'She's only human,' Baxter said, pouring his miniature wine into a plastic glass and bashing its dull edge against Greg's can. 'Cheers, my boy,' he said, as Greg raised his, and took another swig as the train began to slow down.

'It's been happening all day,' Greg said.

Baxter shrugged. He too had noticed the attention, but had chosen to ignore it.

'We're probably marked as missing. On the lam!' he said with a cackle. 'They shall say I kidnapped you.'

Greg guffawed.

Greg had been sad to leave Paris, but for the first time in a long time felt excited at the prospect of returning home. On his journey he had acquired six fridge magnets, three postcards, a bottle of vodka for Suzanne, two hundred cigarettes for Ramila and a Toblerone for his dad; yet he had also left something behind, too. It was as though whatever stone had held tight around his leg since his brother's death had come loose. He was not yet healed, but at long last he was ready for the healing to begin. He felt poised and he felt infinite, facing in the right direction for the first time in as long as he could remember. Life was his for the taking and he was ready for whatever would come his way.

Fortunately their change at King's Cross had been a short one. Baxter had yelled blue murder when Greg had claimed an urgent need for the toilet and hot-tailed it into the crowds with their luggage, leaving Baxter seething beneath the departure boards.

When Greg had eventually returned Baxter had launched into a tirade that lasted all the way to the platform. 'Fat lot of good you are as any sort of packhorse. I wouldn't have minded if you'd left me the bags. I'd have jettisoned you as dead weight to catch the train, believe you me. But off you shot with my personals. I'd half a mind to notify transport police . . .' he said.

'This is our carriage!' Baxter had yelled as Greg shook his head. 'Come on, they'll go without us.'

Greg smiled and handed Baxter the tickets.

'We're up the top now, you miserable old sod,' he had said. 'It was payday when we were away. I upgraded to first class when I was at the loo,' he said, as the old man stifled his elation. 'My way of saying thank you, or whatever.'

'Well,' Baxter said, taking the tickets and slipping them into the pocket of his jacket, 'that is very kind. After worrying me so. Come on, or we'll be the only bloody first-class ticket holders walking home.'

Back at the house Teddy had washed and changed Greg's bedding, and opened the window to air out his room.

News of Greg's sudden departure had reached him via Suzanne and the very next day he had read in the newspaper of the old man's flight of fancy, along with his teenage cohort. Though he was ribbed about it at work, he felt a strange sense of awe at his son's ability to follow his instincts. Teddy's life had been lived to schedule. He was not so much scared of the alternative as oblivious as to its existence. He was pleased, secretly, that his eldest child seemed not to be limited in this way. Somehow, Greg had a mind of his own – and though it would bemuse him for ever, he was no less proud.

When Teddy heard that the pair were on their way back home, he had cleared the garden of the broken crockery and smashed glass from the last night he had spent with his son and, fortified by eight cans of lager, spent a long evening constructing an admirably solid table right in the middle of the yard. Teddy had spent eighteen years yearning for peace, only to find it an empty gift, and one he was keen to return. The house without Greg was unfamiliar and cold. From the big kitchen drawer, he had located a generic greetings card that he had written out in his own spidery scrawl:

Greg,

Welcome home.

Glad you're safe. There's a sandwich in the fridge if you want, and a box of crisps in the back cupboard.

See you tonight.

Dad.

He had placed the card on the boy's fresh pillow, and made his way to work.

Winnifred, Ramila and Suzanne were not the only ones to have arrived on the concourse to witness Baxter's triumphant return. However, the trio were as yet entirely oblivious of this fact, having moved onto a shared bottle of Sauvignon Blanc.

A small crowd was gathering. Two reporters from sparring national newspapers checked the arrival boards and chatted awkwardly on mobile phones. A group of teenagers from the sixth form college, including Charlotte and her cohorts, held pride banners. There was even a local television crew, and three old men in uniform who waited patiently and smartly next to a modest brass band, ready to greet Baxter with an official welcome.

'The train gets in at ten past, but there's works at Chester-le-Street so it might be a bit late,' said one of the reporters.

The train relieved itself of at least half of its passengers as they paused at Durham.

'Lovely, isn't it?' Baxter said, nodding towards the cathedral in the distance as Greg opened one last can to carry him home.

He looked out at the window and shrugged.

'It's all right, I suppose,' he said drily. 'Shit compared to Paris though, isn't it?'

'A jaded traveller after just the one trip!' Baxter said, pouring some of Greg's beer into his own glass, having made his way through the selection of miniatures that had seen him comfortably from Peterborough. 'You've been spoiled,' he added as Greg laughed and nodded in agreement.

'What you thinking?' he asked as the train passed through a tunnel and the sudden blast of light as they emerged caused them both to squint.

'Oh,' Baxter mused, 'nothing you would understand.'

'I'm not as dumb as I look.'

'This is true, Gregory. Go on then, blow my mind. What are *you* thinking?'

Greg had felt a gentle tug of apprehension all morning. 'I was thinking . . .'

Greg strained for a joke, or a jibe, or some way to underplay the discomfort he felt, but stopped himself. *Fuck it,* he thought. *Why bother? You owe him the respect of your honesty at least.*

'I was just thinking that these last few days have been some of the best of my life. You're an awkward old sod and I want to be just like you,' Greg said with a sad laugh.

Baxter smiled at the boy, lost for words.

'I'm serious. You're exactly what I need to be. You make big things seem small and small things seem big and—' he tried desperately, 'and I know you've been sad and hurt. But you've never let it defeat you. You've never been *stuck*. You've always been bigger than the sadness, better than it. It's just this thing inside you, and I want to know how to be that way too.'

'Seems to me,' Baxter said slowly, and careful to keep his own

244

emotions in check, 'that you've already learned how. You're so much cleverer than I was at your age, Gregory. So much stronger than I was when I grieved for Thomas.'

'Yeah, maybe. But I want to be better,' said Greg, shaking his head. 'And it pisses me off, because I wasn't supposed to want that. I was fine before I met you. But the person I was then doesn't feel like enough now. I don't want to be scared like Michael or forgotten like Thomas or angry like Dad. I want to try things that scare me. I want my own adventures. I want to say yes,' he said, his eyes wet now, 'and it's all your fault, Baxter. It's all your fault. So . . . thank you.'

Baxter stretched his hand across the table and gripped the boy tightly as they passed over the water, where the bridges aligned, and they knew they were home.

They waited in the vestibule as the train stopped to allow for the lines to clear just metres from the station.

'Bloody typical,' Baxter moaned from the bathroom where he smoothed his hair in the useless mirror with the tortoiseshell comb. 'You get all the way back from Paris and there's a delay not ten yards from home. Lord have mercy.'

'You look very dapper,' Greg said to Baxter, who joined him by the door and shrugged.

'Presentation is key,' he replied as the engines started up again. 'You'd do well to remember that. *Here*,' he said, handing him the comb, 'you keep it. Mustn't let standards slip, old boy.'

Greg placed the comb into the outer pocket of his bag.

'Thanks, Baxter,' he said.

'Just promise me you'll look after it. It'll make you into quite the gentleman if you treat it right.' Baxter held onto the rail beside the door with one hand as he placed another on Greg's shoulder. 'Come now,' he said as Greg sniffed quietly and swallowed hard on his tears. 'What's all this?'

'I don't know,' he said truthfully. 'I'm not sad. It's just . . . back to real life, isn't it?'

The train began to inch forward slowly towards its destination.

'It's what you make of it. Believe you me.'

'I just want to take what I can get.'

'What a lucky man you are,' Baxter said eventually. 'You have such a big adventure ahead of you.'

'It's scary,' Greg whispered as Baxter nodded in agreement.

'Anything worth doing is.'

Greg wiped his sleeve across his face and cleared his throat.

'Do you feel lucky?' he asked the old man. 'I mean really?'

Baxter thought for a while. He felt each agony and ecstasy pass through him in a surge that made his legs weaken beneath him. Life, it is safe to say, had been exhausting. The entire thing seemed just a messy cacophony; a song played once that could never be repeated. And yet given the chance, he'd do it again in a heartbeat, without changing one moment, whether or not he could survive it a second time over.

'I do feel lucky, Gregory. I think I am the luckiest man there is,' he said with certainty. And Greg smiled, for he believed him.

Winnifred, Suzanne and Ramila made their way from the bar on loose legs and juddering wheels. Their friendship had been cemented by afternoon drinking and the shared love of a dear man. Winnifred had even been tempted to enquire about her own lodgings at Melrose Gardens, but thought better of it for that moment at least, until Baxter decided where his final days would be spent.

'I do feel a bit pissed actually,' Ramila conceded, linking arms with Suzanne as Winnifred swerved the passers-by as best she could.

'I'm arseholed,' Suzanne agreed, squinting to make sense of the station she had walked through a hundred times before. 'I'm going to need some chips or something to sober up. I've got to start the tea yet.'

They stood beneath the departure boards and scanned the information that swirled before their eyes.

'Nonsense,' Winnifred said. 'We've just got started, and my beloved has returned. We shall make a night of it!'

Ramila and Suzanne shot each other a concerned look, before following the old lady who had rolled off towards the waiting crowd.

'What's all this?' Suzanne asked as Winnifred was greeted with a hug by the reporter who had interviewed her just days earlier.

'They must be here for the boys!' Winnifred said.

'It's here!' yelled one of the reporters.

'They're home!' said another.

'You excited to see your fella?' Ramila asked, bending down and hugging Winnifred from behind.

'Relieved. I'd be lost without him.' She said, as Suzanne reached down and took her hand in hers.

It was too late for lunch and too early for rush hour, and yet the station felt electric with life.

'That's that then,' Greg said solemnly, as the crowd dripped past.

'Nonsense,' said Baxter. 'It was merely the beginning. There's plenty more adventures to be had.'

A gentle tap on the elbow interrupted him.

'Excuse me, love,' said a cleaner meekly, as Baxter and Greg scanned the vicinity for the easiest way out. 'You're him, aren't you? The man from the paper?'

Baxter rolled his eyes and fiddled in his pocket to retrieve the tickets for the barriers.

'There's a crowd waiting for you,' she said excitedly, as Baxter handed Greg his bag and rested his weight on his walking stick.

'As well there should be,' he said jubilantly. 'Gregory and I are jewels in this city's crown. I'm surprised it's lasted this long without us, truth be told.'

'I think what you've done is so lovely,' she said warmly. 'Welcome home, anyway. I'm pleased you're safe and sound.'

She made her way with her trolley, leaving Greg and Baxter all but alone on the platform.

'You want to go and see what all that was about?' Greg asked uneasily.

Baxter shook his head. 'Not particularly,' he said wearily, suddenly desperately thirsty and in need of a seat.

'Shall we just get ourselves home then?' asked Greg.

'Always in such a hurry,' Baxter said, gripping his walking stick as he marched Greg towards the bridge connecting the platform to the main drag of the station. 'Let's get a drink and see where the day takes us. There's no rush, is there?' he said, the boy following in his wake, as somewhere in the distance a brass band began to play. And the world was filled with music.

Acknowledgements

Thanks to my family – Mam, Dad, Annie, Nigel and Sophie – and friends, especially Nicole, Sammy and Jess.

Thanks to KC, always.

Thanks to all at Corsair and Little, Brown, which still gives me a thrill to type, and to Olivia Hutchings, Hayley Camis, and Becca Allen.

Special thanks, as always, to Broo Doherty and Sarah Castleton. A dream team for any author, and one I'm lucky enough to call my own. Without them this book would never have happened.